Banking on Murder

Banking on Murder

DAVID BOWRA

IGUANA

Copyright © 2021 David Bowra
Published by Iguana Books
720 Bathurst Street, Suite 303
Toronto, ON M5S 2R4

Publisher: Meghan Behse
Editor: Amanda Feeney
Front cover design: Ruth Dwight, www.designplayground.ca

ISBN 978-1-77180-499-8 (paperback)
ISBN 978-1-77180-500-1 (epub)

This is an original print edition of *Banking on Murder*.

For Daphne

Chapter 1

George Koehle looked around the boardroom with glass walls and leather chairs. He picked a chair three seats away from the door, and it squeaked slightly when he sat on it. He rubbed his hands on his thighs and tried to calm his breathing. His company had banked with Henry Elliott for over fifteen years. Goldstate Finance was an important client and George knew they'd made the bank a lot of money. That calmed him a bit.

And Goldstate had made George a lot of money too. He'd grown the business from scratch into a mid-sized mortgage-investment corporation by attracting investors from his wife's church, who were lured by the promise of high returns. He'd even expanded into Hawaii and then started financing development properties. Then some of the development loans turned bad.

Henry had warned George that the account could be transferred to the Special Loans Group if he kept missing interest payments. But George assumed he could bluff his way out of it, the way he had in the past. Only now Henry wanted to meet with him. A chance to catch up, he'd said. But George hadn't slept well last night. Maybe the bank knew about the bad loans.

George turned toward the door as his old friend walked into the boardroom. "Sorry to keep you waiting, George." Henry was smiling, but George noticed the older man avoided eye contact; he just made his way to the other side of the big table and sat down opposite him. He scratched his silver head with a tired hand before finally looking up at George. "Head office are taking over your account. I told them I wanted to give you the news."

George swallowed hard and felt a sharp pain in his stomach. He rubbed his sweaty hands against his tweed pants again and coughed a little before answering. "Your money is safe. I just need ... a little more time to catch up, just a few weeks."

Henry's blue eyes were gentle. "It's out of my hands. The bank's calling the loan, but said they'd work with you."

The hole in George's stomach got bigger.

Henry reached across his desk and handed George a letter. George wiped a hand across his forehead, took a deep breath and unfolded the document: *Demand loan thirty-five million plus interest, personal guarantee five million.* He looked up at Henry, blinking at the bright light coming from the window behind the banker. "You don't know what you're doing. I'm begging you ... just a few more weeks, please."

Henry stood up, walked to the other side of the desk and put his hand on George's shoulder. "I'm sorry. This is tough for me too; we go back a long way."

"How much time do I have to get the money?"

"It depends on what the consultant says. A guy from Kinsey will call you."

George folded the letter and stuffed it in his jacket pocket. He gave Henry a weak smile before pushing his chair back and standing.

"You'll be okay, George," Henry said. George hesitated before heading through the door, half turned and nodded, then walked quickly to the elevator, staring at the blue carpet all the way down the hall. On the street outside, as he walked back to his office a few blocks away, it came flooding back. That moment twenty years ago when he realized his first business had failed. The shame. The fears that kept him awake so many nights. The things he couldn't share with Thelma, so many things he wanted to tell her as she lay there beside him, breathing peacefully, blissfully ignorant. And now it was happening again. *They're going to shut me down. I'm going to lose everything. My business, my house, Thelma. And what the heck am I going to tell Davis?*

***

The next day, at about four o'clock, the accountant from Kinsey arrived at the small one-storey retail strip mall near the corner of Hastings and Victoria, where George Koehle's offices were located in East Vancouver. Paul Bolton parked his blue Camaro behind the building, took a quick glance in the rear-view mirror and ran his fingers through his blond hair before getting out. He popped a piece of chewing gum in his mouth and gnawed on it aggressively for the minute or so it took to get to the door, then spit it out before entering.

In the small reception area, he was greeted by a young woman who looked up from her computer as he entered. He flashed her a smile, said hello and enjoyed her reaction to his British accent. Bolton leaned on the receptionist's counter to await his appointment, and she didn't seem to mind at all. After a few minutes, a middle-aged man, a little over five foot six, came through a panelled door on the other side of the room. His bald head was glistening beneath the fluorescent lights and Bolton noticed the dark fringe of hair around his ears was slicked back with some kind of cream or, perhaps, sweat.

"I'm George Koehle. Why don't we go into the boardroom?" George led the way down a narrow hall, his shoulders shrugged, as if to say, *Do we really have to do this?*

When they entered the boardroom, another man was already seated at the long rectangular table. Despite his huge frame in the regular-sized chair, the man appeared relaxed, leaning back casually. Though, his dark eyes, fixed on Bolton, made the accountant feel like he was being x-rayed. George beelined to the water cooler on the far side and guzzled from a small cup before turning to face them both. "This is my controller, Alan Davis," he said, his eyes darting between the two men. Bolton reached out with a large hand, then let it drop to his side when Davis just nodded in greeting. George tossed his cardboard cup into the garbage bin and pulled out a chair, motioning for Bolton to do the same.

Bolton sat and set his leather briefcase on the table. "Thanks for meeting me," he said. "The bank's keen on starting the review. Here's a copy of the letter from the bank. It requires your consent."

George skimmed over the eight-page letter. "Can I look at it over the weekend and get back to you Monday?" He passed the letter to Davis, and the big man leaned forward, glanced at the first few pages and then back at Bolton.

Bolton smiled. "Of course. You might have your lawyer review it as well." He handed George another document. "And this is the information we're going to need from you before we start."

George scanned the document and made a sort of huffing sound in the back of his throat. Bolton noticed his eyes widen. "Geez … that's a lot of information, you really need all this stuff?" Bolton couldn't help but notice the way the little man's eyes kept darting back to his controller.

George looked up in time to see Bolton run a careless hand through his hair, and he suddenly remembered what it was like to be that young again, though perhaps he'd never been as carefree as this young man. Certainly not as handsome. He resisted the urge to touch his own remaining wisps.

"It's all fairly routine, Mr. Koehle," Bolton said. "I would expect Mr. Davis here has most of it already." Still silence from the controller who took the paper from George and set it in the pile in front of him, his eyes never leaving Bolton's face.

"Looks like you thought of everything." George straightened up in his chair, his pudgy hands holding the document. "This will take a while to put together. And I better get the lawyer to look it. Why don't I call you when we're ready?"

"It'll be better if I call you, see how you're doing and make sure we can start as soon as possible." Bolton looked at Davis. "Any questions?" Davis barely shook his head, but it was enough. "Righto. Look forward to seeing you soon. If you have any questions, call me anytime." Bolton got up and shook George's hand before the other man had a chance to rise. Then he gathered his things and headed out, flashing a final smile at the receptionist on his way out the door.

***

Half an hour later, George and Davis entered Café Davanis. There were still people at the office and Davis didn't want to be overheard. He ordered two coffees and pointed to a table in the corner. George sat down.

Davis stared at the small man across from him and gritted his teeth. He knew George was a lousy businessman, he just hadn't realized how lousy he was when he'd gotten involved with him three years earlier. Lately, he was taking up too much of Davis's time, and there was still way too much debt. And way too much at stake. Davis thought of what his boss's reaction would be when he'd explained the situation. Walter McVittie was not a patient man at the best of times. His plan to run cash through George's business had seemed surefire. They'd done it dozens of times with the travel agency, the clubs and the pubs. And they were always able to get their money out if the business had to close down. Businesses that needed ongoing funding were bad news for the gang, and they usually let them go bankrupt. They'd shut the place down, destroy all the records and walk away.

George looked at Davis and, as usual, couldn't read the man's face. He noticed the owner of the coffee shop looking at them, so he leaned forward and kept his voice low. "What do you think? I'm worried about my investors, what's going to happen to them? Can't you put any more money in and buy us some more time with the bank?"

Davis scowled and scratched at a scar just above his right eye. "Not gonna happen. And the bank will decide what happens to the investors."

A waitress brought their coffees, and for a moment, George was occupied filling his with cream and sugar. Davis took a sip of his coffee and set the cup down, staring into the dark liquid. If George was running a small operation, like a pub, then maybe more money would work. But there were too many employees, friggin' private investors and a bank with a lot of debt. He closed his eyes for a moment and opened them to find George staring at him, his watery eyes intent. "It had made sense as a short-term loan, but that was three years ago, George." McVittie was right. They should've got out a long time ago. Davis had broken his cardinal rule: Never get involved in a business with too much debt.

George opened and closed his mouth like a fish. "But … but I—"

But Davis had made up his mind. This meeting was pointless. It was damage-control time now. He stood up. "We can't have any of this coming back on us, you get me, George? Get your shit together, come up with a story for the staff and get rid of them."

"Um … a story?" George was staring up at Davis with glossy eyes.

"Tell 'em you're going to Hawaii to sell some properties or raise some money. And shut the office for two weeks."

"What about the payroll?"

Davis pulled some bills out of his wallet and tossed them on the table. "They'll get paid till the end of the month."

"We don't have enough cash. The cheques will bou—"

"Christ, George. Do I look like I care?" George couldn't hold Davis's penetrating stare and looked away. "Besides, it won't be the first time you lied. That Bolton guy will be back asking questions and the bank's not letting this go. We ain't gonna be around when the shit hits the fan. Shut the place down now, get rid of the records and disappear. Now let's go. We've got some planning to do."

***

At home that evening, Davis leaned back into his black leather couch and took a sip of his favourite single malt whisky. *Goddam George*

Koehle, he thought. This was the last thing he needed. And now McVittie was pushing again, looking for more ways to make money. And what did he do all day? Davis was the one who came up with all the ideas. He was the one who made them money. McVittie just sat on his fat ass and drank. Davis took another slug of whisky. *How the hell did I end up working for someone like him?*

Davis was young when he'd drifted into the gang. Back then, there didn't seem to be any other way. And he was smart, so he'd risen through the ranks, become the financial mastermind, helped McVittie expand into the legal and not so legal. And it wasn't so bad, when he considered the money he'd made. But in the end, it had cost him. The day his wife walked out and took his daughter, the day she told him she couldn't stand the life anymore, he wasn't worth it … He hadn't seen either of them in over ten years.

Did he really see himself working for McVittie twenty years from now?

Davis stared out the window. Maybe George wasn't a problem … but an opportunity to change his life, to leave the gang. Davis closed his eyes and leaned back. No one left the gang. He set his glass down and sighed. He was stuck, and now he had to clean up George's mess too.

Chapter 2

George was terrified. He had to tell his wife about the business. She knew something was wrong. He got hardly any sleep that weekend. And she'd asked him a dozen times. Most recently that morning at breakfast. But he couldn't say the words. Couldn't let her down again. He'd lied, as usual, then left the house as quickly as possible.

George stared into the bathroom mirror and pressed a few wisps of dark hair against his pale skull. Why would she stay? Why would anyone stay with him? Sooner or later, he'd have to tell her how bad it really was. He clutched the white sink with two hands and leaned forward heavily, his breath coming in sharp little gasps. *Stay calm. Slow breaths.* He tried to remember what they taught him at the hospital last time. *Last time.* When he'd lost it all. When he'd lived in a mental ward for months. And this was so much worse. This time he'd convinced Thelma to ask members of their church to invest. What if he lost all their money? They'd turn their backs on her. She'd have to leave the church. And Thelma would never forgive him for that.

The door to the men's room opened and George straightened up, cleared his throat and adjusted his tie. He nodded to the other man, then left the washroom and went back down the hall to his office to pick up a few files. He'd asked all the staff to go to the boardroom for a short meeting. They were waiting. He wondered what he should tell them and realized he'd probably end up lying yet again. He took a moment to stare at the picture of Thelma, her short brown hair blowing across her plain pink face, that smile he loved so much, the one that seemed to reach her eyes so easily. She'd always been like that. No pretense. You got what you saw. Most guys wouldn't notice her, but they didn't know what they were missing.

As he walked to the boardroom with a file folder under his arm, he could hear chatter. Probably the staff wondering if they were going to get paid. He sat down at the head of the table and looked around the room. They were used to the ups and downs of the business. He played with the folder and pretended to open it. Then he looked at the staff that had been there the longest. "As you know," he began, his voice higher than intended. Then he smiled, a quick little break to catch his breath, and continued in a lower voice, "Cash is really tight. The real estate markets have slowed down. Alan Davis and I are going to Hawaii."

That raised some eyebrows. A few people began to ask questions too, but George put his hands up in front of him, his invisible barrier. *Just a few more minutes*, he thought. "We're going to sell some properties. We'll be gone about ... two weeks."

Some of the staff nodded. They knew things were tight. There'd been calls from investors looking for their overdue dividend payments.

George felt strangely encouraged. "To, uh, preserve cash, I plan to close the office for a few weeks."

A few people put up their hands. But George needed to get through this quickly or he might not make it. He could feel the heat around his collar and in his armpits. "Now, we have enough cash to cover the payroll. And I'll be back in two weeks, and we'll figure out where we go from there. Think of it as a ... a paid vacation."

Hands shot up again. This time they didn't wait for permission.

"What about calls from investors?"

"How do we reach you in an emergency?"

"What do we say to the investors if we see them at church?"

George pulled on his collar. Why had he worn this blasted wool vest? He didn't have answers to their questions and just said the first thing that came into his head. "Refer them to Thelma." Another lie. His wife hadn't worked at the company in over three years. Anxious to get the meeting over, he stood up awkwardly, almost fell backwards when his chair didn't push out as expected, but recovered, and gathered his papers together somewhat clumsily. "Uh, okay if there are no more questions, I'll see you all in … in two weeks." Then he turned and walked out of the room, ignoring the raised hands and a few voices behind him.

He shut the door to his office and, on impulse, locked it. Thelma was still staring up at him from the picture frame on his desk. She'd probably heard some rumours at church already. She was probably worried about the investors too. This morning, before he rushed off, he told her not to answer any calls at home because there were a few problems at work. *Was that the best I could come up with?* he thought. He left before she could question another of his lies. He'd have to tell her about the staff meeting. Some of the women in the office would see her at church. She'd find out anyway. But he wasn't good at lying to her. She could always see through him.

For the rest of the day, George put off talking to Thelma. In the end, he called her and left a message telling her that he and Alan Davis were going to Hawaii to sell some properties. He didn't mention anything about her going to the office while he was away. And he was grateful she wasn't there to question him.

Chapter 3

On Friday, Paul Bolton called George's office several times, but there was no answer. Finally, around five o'clock, he drove out to the company's offices. It was a typical late-October day in Vancouver, cold and wet. When he arrived, the front door was locked and there were no lights on. He banged on the door several times and cursed under his breath. He walked around the back and found the parking lot empty and the back door locked. Once again, he banged. No response. He checked at the dry cleaners next door and the Indian restaurant on the other side. No one had seen George Koehle that day. And the restaurant owner told him he was pretty sure he hadn't seen any of the employees who usually came in for lunch during the week.

Bolton thought about walking a few blocks to see if the banker was still in his office, but it was raining, so he called Henry Elliott from a pay phone.

"I hope nothing has happened to him," Henry said when he heard what Bolton had to say. "George doesn't always share things, and maybe they're worse than we thought."

Bolton sensed Henry was holding something back. "Mr. Elliott, is there something you're not telling me?"

"Well, as you know, George's company has had some problems, missed interest payments, it's overdrawn and has too much debt. And, well, we've had to return all the payroll cheques … overdraft rules, you see."

I bet the wanker's skipped town, Bolton thought. "Well, I'll keep trying to find him. In the meantime, I'll order title searches of the company's properties. I'll get back to you once they come in."

***

On Monday afternoon, Bolton called the bank again. "Mr. Elliott, I've got the title searches back for the Canadian properties. Every bloody one has been transferred to private individuals." He read out the names and told him the properties had a combined value of about twenty-five million dollars. "Are you still there?"

"Sorry, I was just trying to take it all in. Those people are all members of George's Jehovah's Witness church. They're his investors. Harry Choi is the company's accountant. Garry Steiner is the company's lawyer. I'm going to have to call you back. I need to speak to head office."

***

The next day, Elliott met Bolton in the lobby of the bank's third-floor head office. He introduced the young accountant to the bank's special credit officer, Andrew Bates, and their lawyer, Steve Yensen. The four men walked silently to a small boardroom off the main reception area.

They'd barely sat down when Bates, a pit bull of a man, leaned forward and glared around the table at them all. "So, George Koehle took matters into his own hands, it seems. I bet the US properties have been transferred as well." His glare landed on Henry Elliott, who'd avoided making eye contact with him up till now, as if it was his fault that the assets had disappeared. Bates then turned to Yensen. "So, what can we do?"

The bank was a relatively new client for Yensen's firm, and he was anxious to create a favourable impression. "The bank could petition the company into bankruptcy and commence proceedings to have the property transfers voided and the assets returned to the company."

Bates stared at him. "So, assuming we're successful in getting the properties back, the bank would be entitled to keep all the proceeds?"

"Well ... I'll need to look into that and get back to you." Yensen hadn't thought of that and regretted being so quick to come up with an answer.

"Forgive me," said Bates as he scowled at Yensen. "Maybe you should find out before we go to the trouble and expense of recovering all the assets." Bates turned his gaze on Bolton. "Would getting the Mounties involved help us in any way?"

Bolton adjusted his dark-red tie and unbuttoned his jacket. "There's no doubt they could open doors that a trustee in bankruptcy couldn't. They'd be able to examine the controller, Davis, and the company's external accountant and lawyer, even the investors. The threat of criminal proceedings might make them more cooperative."

Bates smiled for the first time and looked at Yensen. "When can we expect to hear back from you with some answers?"

"I'll get something to you this evening."

Bates stood up, indicating the meeting was over.

When Bolton got back to his office, he found the US property searches on his desk. He quickly reviewed them and discovered they'd all been transferred to individual investors as well. He phoned Yensen and gave him the news.

"I just had a call with Garry Steiner, the Goldstate lawyer," Yensen told him. "I asked him about the recent property transfer from the company to his law firm. He hesitated, then said that it was for services rendered and services to be rendered. When I asked him to explain what 'services to be rendered' means, he hung up."

Bolton was quiet. Yensen didn't want to be blamed if things didn't work out. Many of the US properties were subject to prior mortgages, maintenance fees and property taxes, and he doubted the company had been paying those bills.

"Listen, Paul, if the bank is going to act, it needs to act quickly."

"Do you really think they're going to want to litigate in the US?" Bolton asked. In his experience, fees for litigation in the US could easily run to hundreds of thousands of dollars, especially if you had to file bankruptcy proceedings there as well. And there was no guarantee the assets would be recovered. What law firm would take on the litigation on a contingency basis?

Yensen didn't argue with him.

"Look, mate," Bolton said, "the Canadian assets offer a better chance of recovery, and the litigation costs can be controlled better here. I'm not convinced that the bank will fund litigation to recover the US properties." Bolton waited for a response from Yensen. But the other man stayed silent. Bolton sighed. "Then there's the public relations issue. What do you think the media and the public are going to make of a bank suing a group of retired churchgoers who've invested their life savings in this company? It's just not cricket. The public wouldn't care if it was fraud. They'll have no sympathy for the bank. It'll be eaten alive in the press."

Yensen rubbed a hand over his face. "Good point. Look, I better go and finish this memo. Thanks, you've been a great help." Yensen hung up. He hadn't thought of that. Some things were best left unsaid or, at the very least, not put in writing.

Later that day, Bolton received another call from Yensen. "I just got off the phone with Bates. Paul, I have to be honest, I hadn't thought of the public relations issue, and neither had Bates. I missed it completely, you saved my bacon and I want to thank you."

"No problem, mate. So, what's Bates going to do?"

"I think the plan is to avoid a public relations nightmare—he's going to kick it upstairs. This is way above his pay grade."

Chapter 4

After lying to his wife about going to Hawaii, things had only gotten worse for George Koehle. As Davis had instructed him to do, he'd brought a small suitcase to work with him on the Monday he'd shut down his office, but he hadn't really thought he'd need it. Then on Tuesday morning, after spending a miserable night on Davis's couch, he'd been roused early and told to get in the car, which he did, of course, though he didn't know where they were going. When he asked, Davis told him he needed to hide him somewhere for a few weeks until he developed a plan. And the last thing he needed was George talking to the bank or even the police. Davis said his cabin near Anahim Lake in central BC was the perfect place. Far from anywhere, no phone, no neighbours.

George was quiet during the trip, and Davis used the time during the ten-hour drive to reflect on his life. He thought back to the time before he'd joined the gang. Fresh out of school, he'd gotten a job with a private security company. They had taught him how to search for bugs in people's homes and businesses. Then he became a bodyguard and was licensed as a private investigator. One night, he was approached by a guy in a bar and asked to do some private work sweeping his home and business for bugs. One job led to another and soon he had a few private clients, but he didn't always know who he was dealing with.

One evening, he had been working a private security detail, covering a fancy downtown fundraiser. The RCMP surveillance sweep checked all personnel covering the event and discovered he'd done some work for gang members. The RCMP cancelled his private investigator licence, told his boss about his gang contacts and threatened to cancel their licence as well if they didn't fire him. Davis was out of a job. At the time, he wondered if he'd been set up. Then one of the gang members offered him some work selling cocaine. He had told himself it was temporary. Christ, what had he been thinking?

The gang's idea of making money was to redistribute drugs in small parcels and sell them to dealers. And they had interests in a few small businesses. Davis thought there were better ways to make money. He didn't know much about business, so he started reading. He studied finance and accounting and developed a network of brokers and commercial realtors selling small businesses. Some of their clients were looking for investors to finance or expand their operations.

It would often start as a high-interest loan, and after a while, when the owner couldn't pay, they'd take over the business. He helped the gang acquire several of these businesses, including pubs, a nightclub, a loan company for people with poor credit and a used-car financing company. Gradually he was spending less time delivering coke and more time overseeing businesses and looking for new ones to acquire.

Managing so many different businesses was stressful, and he started to put on weight and exercise less. He even thought he was being followed by the police. One morning, the Vancouver Police Emergency Task Force broke into his house, and he was arrested. They took him away in handcuffs. He'd been arrested before, but he'd never been to jail. They arrested ten other gang members too. At the time, he remembered thinking that these guys who always looked so tough somehow looked different in prison. Now he saw them as others did, with their beer guts, untidy appearance and lack of personal hygiene. Some of them looked like they belonged in a drunk tank or a homeless shelter.

They were all charged with conspiracy to traffic cocaine and were denied bail. But after just twenty days in prison, most of them were let out and the charges were stayed. Davis knew there was enough evidence for a conviction, but, for whatever reason, he was set free. But it didn't matter. When he got out, the woman he loved was gone. And she'd taken their daughter with her.

He'd been happy working his security job and making a few extra bucks on the side. Now he had no life, no career, no family. And the only thing he could do was keep working for the gang. He was trapped.

***

The drive to the cabin had been difficult. There were icy patches along Highway 97 and a few heavy snow flurries. Not that it was a problem for the Land Rover. When they reached the cabin, it was already dark. There was a light dusting of snow on the ground. Davis told George to stay in the vehicle and used his flashlight to go to the barn, unlock the door, and turn on the generator. The inside of the fifty-year-old log cabin was as cold as the outside. He'd planned to make some upgrades but never seemed to have the time.

Davis was pleased to see that his neighbour, Roy Long Feathers, had left some firewood by the front door. Cold as it was, the cabin always felt like home, and all of Davis's troubles were far away in Vancouver. He returned to the vehicle and motioned for George to get out. "Make yourself useful," he said. He tossed George his backpack and then handed him a few bags of groceries.

George stumbled across the slippery driveway carrying the heavy bags. "Well, not ... exactly Hawaii ... is it?" He slipped and caught himself without dropping anything, then turned to Davis, looking rather pleased with himself. "So how long are we going to be here?"

Davis slammed the Land Rover door, his flashlight shining ahead of them. "Long enough to figure out a plan. You've gotta keep a low profile until things settle down on the coast, so this will be home for you for a while, and you better get used to it."

Once inside, George dropped the bags on the counter and let his backpack slip to the floor next to Davis's duffel bag, which was open with a book peeking out. George bent down and picked it up. The title was *No Way Out* and there was a picture of a biker on the back of a Harley. "What's this about?"

Davis swiped the book from him. "Put your stuff in the smaller bedroom. Then you can unpack the groceries and get some coffee on."

As George set his things in the smaller room, Davis lit a fire in the fireplace, but it would be a while before it would start to throw off some heat. George came back into the kitchen and stood by the Aga stove until it was hot and the kettle on it boiling, which took about twenty minutes. He poured water into two mugs of instant coffee, opened a container of cream they'd brought and poured some into his. Then he brought the cups over to the table and sat down.

Davis took his mug of coffee. "So, where are we?" he asked.

George looked up, a little surprised. "In the middle of nowhere, it seems. I didn't see any house lights or cars for at least the last thirty minutes and—"

"I'm talking about Goldstate and the bank." Davis set his coffee down on the table, stood up and opened a nearby cupboard. He pulled out a bottle of blended whisky, uncorked it and poured a generous amount into his coffee.

This was the perfect chance for George to tell Davis about the property transfers. But Davis had made it very clear that George was not to do anything but keep quiet and get rid of his staff for a few weeks. What would Davis say when he found out that George had transferred all the properties to his investors? He realized this would cause the bank to get the police involved. And he dreaded Davis's reaction. He'd go ballistic. *No*, he thought, *now isn't the time to tell him*.

Davis looked over at him as if he were daydreaming. "George, I asked you a question."

George glanced up, startled. He almost blurted it out but caught himself. "I'm, uh, pretty tired from the drive. Can we talk about this tomorrow?" He stood up and did a sort of sideways shuffle from the room, his attempt to look casual. "So, good night," he added before turning to head down the hall.

Davis frowned. Was there something George wasn't telling him?

***

Davis was up early the following morning. He sat on a bench outside and breathed in the cold fresh air through his nose. He'd been hooked on the area years ago when he came on a fly-fishing trip. He'd missed his trips to the cabin, which had become less frequent as he got busier. The place had everything: the great outdoors, peace and quiet, wide open space, no stress and no one to worry about. He had enough money to live on. If only he could live here. He was dreaming; there was no way he could have this life.

A few hours later, George came outside, hugging himself and rubbing his hands on his arms. "So, what do people do around here?"

Davis pushed himself up from the bench and took his coffee inside with him. "Let me grab my keys," he said. "I'll show you around."

George followed him. "But I haven't had anything to eat yet."

Davis grabbed his wallet and keys off the counter. "There's a restaurant."

After the ten-and-a-half hour drive the previous day, George wasn't keen on jumping back in the car, but he followed Davis outside to the Land Rover, and a few minutes later they were back on the road. Davis held the wheel with one hand, a coffee with the other. They hadn't talked much since they'd left Vancouver. And George had spent a lot of time thinking. Davis had told him he needed to get out of town for a while, "to let the dust settle," but he hadn't really explained why George had to leave the city.

They drove along the snow-covered dirt road and then turned right onto Highway 20. Within minutes, an RCMP vehicle drove past from the opposite direction. George slouched down in his seat a little. Davis looked at him and actually smiled. "Relax, George. They're not looking for you. They're on their way to the reserve."

George looked at Davis and said, "How long do I have to hide? I can't stay here forever."

"Listen, this won't be forever. We just need to lay low till this all blows over. The bank will move in, take over and sell the assets, and that'll be it."

George gave him a weak smile and gazed out the window. He knew things wouldn't blow over, especially when the bank found out about the transfers. He wondered if he'd ever be able to go home. And what about the gang, what the heck would they do? They were still owed some money as well. What a mess, and he still hadn't told Davis about what he'd done with the properties.

Whenever George had bad thoughts, he tried to put them at the back of his mind and focus on pleasant things. It was something they told him to do when he was in the hospital. It worked sometimes, but not for long.

Within a few minutes, he sat up taller and was starting to show some interest in his surroundings. To his great surprise, Davis was a good tour guide. He told George they were on the doorstep of Tweedsmuir Provincial Park, named after John Buchan (Baron Tweedsmuir), who wrote *The Thirty-Nine Steps*. George stared at the gang member he barely knew. This was certainly a side he'd never seen.

Davis looked out the window and said, "Look out there, George. This is home to some of the world's biggest grizzlies and black bears. It's the last true wilderness." George thought he caught a tone of regret or sadness in the other man's voice.

After a few kilometres, they pulled off the highway and into a motel parking lot. "Are you sure this is safe?" George asked, glancing around at the three other parked cars.

"We're in the middle of nowhere. No one's gonna recognize you."

George followed Davis across the gravel lot. "Still … won't the police be looking for—"

"Just act normal and don't draw attention to yourself."

They headed for the restaurant where George counted six people sitting at tables. An elderly couple smiled at them as they walked past. A group of four men, one of whom had some kind of official looking logo on his jacket, were deep in conversation and ignored them. "Those look like cops," George said in a low voice.

"They're from the Forest Service. They're up here all the time lately. Dealing with the pine beetle infestation."

Davis headed to the far end of the restaurant and took a table by the window. The waitress brought over a water jug, filled both their glasses and asked if they wanted coffee. When she returned with the steaming mugs, Davis ordered a ham-and-cheese omelette with a salad. George ordered a burger and fries.

"You gentleman from out of town?"

"The coast. How about you?" said the new, talkative Davis.

"We just moved here from Bella Coola. What brings you here?"

George froze, but Davis just smiled. George realized it was the second time in one day he'd seen more than a smirk on the big man's weathered face. "We're up for few days. Staying in a friend's cabin."

"Where's that?"

"Halfway between here and Nimpo Lake."

"Oh yeah? My husband might know him. What's his name?"

"Martin Becker."

The waitress smiled and walked away. George looked at her as she left, then back at Davis who shrugged. "It's a small town." Davis looked out the window and saw the RCMP cruiser pull in.

The two Mounties came in and sat at a table a few booths down. One made eye contact with Davis, who smiled and nodded. The cop nodded back. The waitress served their meal, then walked over to another table to pick up some dishes and chat with the Mounties. Davis glared at George. "Calm down. They're not talking about us. They're having lunch."

Davis took his time eating; George couldn't finish his meal quickly enough. Davis held his cup up and signalled to the waitress for another coffee. She came by with the pot, smiled at them and moved to another table, pouring more coffee. After a few minutes, Davis caught the waitress's attention and made a signal as if he were signing a cheque. She brought the bill over and he paid in cash, the tip no more than ten per cent of the bill.

Davis headed for the door, George right behind, avoiding eye contact with any of the diners. They got in the Land Rover and drove back onto the highway, heading northwest along Highway 20 toward Tweedsmuir Provincial Park.

"Where are we going now?" George asked.

"You wanna stay in the cabin all day?" George thought that was sort of the point of coming up here: to hide out. Davis glanced at him and it was as though he could read his mind. "No one's going to notice you up here. We're in the middle of nowhere. And I want to show you the lodge."

The drive to the lodge would take about an hour and a half. Davis glanced at his watch; it was 1:30 p.m. He wasn't sure how far he wanted to drive, especially since he'd had a long drive the night before.

As they continued down the highway, Davis explained that the area was home to one of the highest waterfalls in Canada and Canada's second-highest mountain, Mount Waddington, at just over four thousand metres. The valley they were driving through was home to giant coastal hemlock, western red cedar, and Douglas fir, many over seventy metres tall. Again, George was amazed at this change in Davis, who usually didn't say this much in a whole day.

A few minutes later, they pulled off the highway at the sign Ulkatcho First Nation.

"This is the lodge?" George asked.

"Nope. Too late to go to the lodge today. This is a pit stop. I have to drop a book off."

As they followed the dirt road into the reserve, Davis began talking about his friend, Roy Long Feathers. After about ten minutes, they reached a series of small, one-storey buildings, the cleanest and newest of which was the band office.

When they got out of the car, Davis turned to George. "Remember these are proud people." George didn't know what that meant, but he followed him to the door of the office, which was opened by a tall, elderly fellow with high cheekbones and long grey hair.

"Alan, how are you?" the old man said as he hugged Davis. George's jaw dropped.

Davis turned toward George. "This is my friend, Roy Long Feathers," he said. George moved forward and shook his hand. He was even taller than Davis.

"Davis—I mean, uh, Alan—tells me you're a band councillor," George said. "He told me all about you."

"I've been a councillor for many years. What exactly has my old friend said?"

George didn't know what to say. Many of the things Davis had told him were not pleasant. George had heard something of residential schools, but he'd never met anyone who'd actually been to one. Davis had told him Roy had been taken from his family when he was child and sent to the residential school near Williams Lake, some three hundred kilometres away.

"Oh, just history. I'm very interested in your history…" George said awkwardly.

Roy smiled. "Then I will tell you more. Come in!" He motioned them forward and headed to the other side of the room where a coffee pot was still warm. "The name of the village means *fat of the land*," he began as he poured out three mugs. He handed one to each man and continued his history lesson. After several moments, his eyes had drifted past them. When he stopped speaking and glanced back at them, he looked as if he'd awoken from a dream. Their coffee mugs were empty. "I could go on for hours. But I sense you are on your way somewhere."

Davis smiled. "We need to get on the road. I just wanted to bring your book back." He laid the borrowed book on the counter next to his mug.

Davis and George thanked Roy and said goodbye. As they got back onto the highway, George turned in his seat a bit. He was thinking about how complicated his life had gotten. "He lives a very simple life, doesn't he?"

Davis glanced at him. "That's what I thought, too, when I first met Roy." Davis bit the inside of his lip. He'd been envious. Roy lived up here all year round. His world was filled with nature and peace. No gang. Davis stared ahead out the windshield. The snow was starting to come down and it was later than he'd intended. "I think we better check out the lodge tomorrow," he said.

"What did you mean, that's what you thought too?" George asked.

Davis was quiet for another moment, then he said, "Once I got to know him, I began to understand what he's been through. I thought my life—" Davis stopped and seemed to be thinking about whether to continue, and, for once, George waited quietly. "Well, his life hasn't been easy. You hear about the white man taking their land and the residential schools, and for us, it's just history. But for Roy, it's like yesterday. He carries it with him everywhere. Everything that's happened to him and his people. It's all there with him, all the time."

George didn't know what to make of this new side of Alan Davis.

***

When they got back to the cabin, Davis was his usual quiet self as he moved around getting things ready for dinner. But while they ate, he opened up again and told George stories about the area and talked about the wildlife surrounding them. George felt almost cheerful as he peppered Davis with questions. While he was pleased that George was starting to relax, Davis knew that either he or someone else from the gang would almost certainly be dealing with George on a permanent basis. He couldn't let his own feelings get in the way. But was that it? That he may be forced to get rid of George?

In bed, Davis had trouble sleeping. He'd been thinking about the gang and what he should do with George. It'd be easier just to worry about himself. He didn't owe George anything. And sooner or later George would screw things up, talk to the police, tell his wife or his son, Karl, about the business. Karl was another problem.

***

George sat at the small wooden table in the kitchen after Davis had gone to bed and wondered how long he'd be staying at the cabin. He'd panicked when the bank called the loan and when Bolton showed up to talk about the business review. And he knew it was only a matter of time before the bank would find out about the property transfers to the investors. When Davis stepped in and told him to shut the place down, he didn't argue. He didn't know what to do. Running away was always an option. He'd done it before. But it was as if he couldn't think. And then Davis took charge, and that made everything easier. George realized that at some point, he'd have to tell Davis about the transfers, even though he knew it would make him angry. He'd do it tomorrow.

George took a sip from his mug and looked around. He was amazed how Davis could live in the old cabin. The only modern feature was the Aga stove. He'd wandered into Davis's bedroom by mistake when they first arrived. It was neat and tidy and there was a framed photo on the bedside table. A thirty-something woman, not unattractive, and a young girl, both smiling. He didn't know Davis had any family. There was a lot he didn't know about the man. And this trip was certainly showing him a side he'd never seen before. Davis appeared to love nature and the outdoors, and his choice of books was unexpected. Philosophy, meditation, yoga, nature, history and crime novels, all in the small bookcase. Maybe they belonged to someone else, the woman in the photo? They certainly didn't strike him as books Davis would read.

Again, George picked up *No Way Out*. He'd started reading it last night, after Davis had gone to bed. It was about a guy from back east who ended up joining a gang. Drug trafficking and other bad stuff. After a few years of rising through the ranks, he decided he wanted out. But there was no way out, unless it was in a wooden box. He ended up becoming a police informant but stayed in the gang, knowing that if he ever got caught, he was a dead man.

George set the book down. Why did he get the feeling that this wasn't too different from Davis's real-life story? He thought about the picture he'd seen of the woman and the little girl. But then another thought slipped into his mind, and he started to feel sick. If Davis was willing to lose his family to be in a gang, was he really the type of guy who'd take care of George? Or had he brought him up here for another reason?

Chapter 5

Bolton had been in his office on Burrard Street since 7:00 a.m. He'd wanted to call his contact at the RCMP Commercial Crime Division in Vancouver for a few days now. They'd worked a major fraud investigation about six months ago, and half a dozen criminals ended up going to prison for several years. Bolton finished his third cup of tea and kept going over in his mind what he was going to say. After waiting as long as he could, he picked up the phone hoping to catch him.

Pat Lossan was glad to hear from his friend, but he had a million things to do that day. He cradled the phone between his ear and shoulder and shuffled a few papers across his desk as Bolton explained the events leading up to the bankruptcy petition and how all the assets had been transferred to investors a few days after the bank called the loan. "Listen, Paul," Lossan said, "This sounds more like a civil matter. I don't know how I can help you. And I'm swamped right now. It's great to hear from you but I've got—"

"Wait." Bolton took a shaky breath. "That's not why I rang you, Pat."

"It's not?"

"No. I've been getting some pretty strange phone calls ... well, threatening phone calls actually. Three of them this past weekend."

"And you think it's related to this fraud case?" Lossan had stopped shuffling papers.

"I don't know. Recently I've been dealing with some dodgy characters, and it could easily be one of them. There's a nightclub owner who's also a drug dealer. And I'm up to my ears in this used-car leasing agency that looks like it's been funded by offshore money. And I've got a local condo developer that the FBI are checking into for fraud. That chap's being extradited to the United States and—"

"Whoa. Slow down. Give me some names, okay?"

Bolton rattled off a few names, and Lossan wrote them down on a yellow legal pad, then frowned. Paul was usually so confident. This didn't sound like him. "Let's meet today. Grab a coffee and we'll talk this through. It's probably all in your head, my friend."

***

An hour later, Bolton walked into the Mounties' offices on Heather Street in Vancouver. Lossan was waiting for him in the lobby, his six-foot-three frame almost as wide as the doorway he was standing in. Bolton thought he wouldn't have looked out of place on a football field. The young Mountie waved a huge hand and called across the lobby in his booming voice, making Bolton relax for the first time in almost a week.

He followed Lossan upstairs and into a small office. Lossan crowded behind a small desk and Bolton sat in the only other chair, across from him. His blue suit was uncharacteristically wrinkled, and he had dark bags under his eyes.

"All right, tell me about these threatening calls. Pretend I'm on the line, tell me what the caller says, word for word."

"All three times, it's been the same. 'I'm going to get you, if it's the last thing I do, I'm going to get you.'" Bolton took a deep breath and ran a careless hand through his hair. Lossan had seen him do that so many times, it would have made him smile if his friend wasn't so upset.

"Describe the voice."

"Male, Canadian, not English or foreign. No accent. It … sounds rehearsed. There's no emotion. It's all over in five seconds, and then he hangs up." Bolton had been looking around the room during this speech, like he couldn't find something to focus on. Now he stared up at Lossan with bloodshot eyes ringed with the kind of dark stain that persists after days of poor sleep.

"When did you get these calls?"

"Saturday morning at about one thirty, again around three, and then Sunday morning at about two fifteen."

"All in the middle of the night." Lossan was mumbling to himself as he took notes. He glanced up at his friend. "Listen, I ran those names you gave me. That nightclub owner, Sam Vachilles—"

Bolton's heart sank. "Don't tell me *he's* after me. That crazy bastard swore he'd get even after we shut him down. And he's a serious drug dealer. He—"

"Paul, take a breath." Lossan's dark eyes were filled with concern. "Vachilles is dead. Overdose a few weeks ago." Bolton sank a little further in his chair, relief on his face as he looked up at his friend. "We'll know soon enough if any of them have a record. And, in the meantime, I don't think it's serious. The caller was just trying to scare you."

"Well, guess what, he succeeded." Bolton dropped his head into his hands and took a few moments to compose himself. "Look, thanks, Pat. I—"

"How about you come look at a few mug shots and—"

"Mug shots?" Bolton looked up at him again. "It's only been phone calls."

"You might have actually seen this guy somewhere and not even realized it."

"You mean, you think he might be following me?"

"Look, Paul, it's simple really. Real villains don't threaten, they act. You could be in a washroom somewhere taking a leak and someone'll just walk up behind you and stick a knife in your back."

"A knife?" Bolton couldn't tell if he was serious. "This isn't helping, mate."

Lossan almost knocked his coffee mug over as he jumped forward to reassure his friend. "No, no, I just meant—I tell you what, just in case, and to put your mind at rest, come look at a few mug shots, see if you recognize anyone." He gave what he hoped was a reassuring smile. "Come on," he said, getting up and walking around the desk. "I'll take you down there."

The two men walked down the hall to an office where Lossan's assistant, Mark, put several large binders of photographs in front of Bolton. "Take your time, Paul, and let me know if you recognize anyone." Lossan left the room.

Bolton had trouble focusing. The photos all started to look the same. *This is a waste of time; I don't recognize any of these tossers.* Then Bolton paused on the second last page of the fourth binder. "This chap. His hair is shorter, but the eyes are the same ... Yeah, I think that's him."

Mark called Lossan, who returned with a coffee in one hand and tea for Bolton in the other. He set the mugs down next to the computer his assistant was tapping at. "Got something?"

Bolton stood up and walked to his friend. "Not my guy, but I recognize someone from a meeting I had with George Koehle. It looks like Alan Davis, the controller from Goldstate. But I'm not a hundred per cent sure."

Mark walked over to the printer, pulled a paper out and handed it to Lossan. Lossan stared at the photo. "He goes by several different names, Davis is one of them. He's also known as Peter Robinson. He's a member of the Reds, a Vancouver gang. Guy's a financial wiz, kind of a money manager for Walter McVittie. You heard of him?"

Bolton shook his head.

"McVittie's a bad actor. We've been watching him for years. Know he's guilty, just can't make anything stick."

Bolton put a hand up. "Wait a minute. You're telling me Goldstate's controller is a gang member?"

"Not just a gang member. He's McVittie's second-in-command."

Bolton looked like he'd been hit with a two-by-four. "But what the hell is he doing with George Koehle?"

Lossan glanced back at the paper he was holding. "Maybe Koehle owed them money."

***

A few days later, Bolton was seated at the back of courtroom number 41 of the British Columbia Supreme Court in Vancouver. He'd worn his favourite striped tie and new black shoes he got that weekend. Lossan thought he looked much more like the Paul from six months ago, and he smiled at him and gave a friendly wave when he walked past and took a seat near the front.

Bolton rarely attended bankruptcy hearings. They were always heard along with other cases, and the judge usually started with the uncontested motions and then moved onto the contested ones. Most bankruptcy hearings were contested. On the few occasions he'd attended before, the hearings seemed to take forever. But this one was personal. There had been no more late-night phone calls, but he felt like the rug could get pulled out from under him again at any time. He leaned forward in his seat, struggling to hear the bank's counsel explain to the court that all attempts to reach George Koehle had failed. Counsel argued that, given all the circumstances, the requirement to show proof of service and adherence to the normal eight-days-notice period should be dispensed with. Several cases were cited where the court had exercised its discretion in situations where there appeared to have been a fraud. The judge nodded a few times and asked a few questions before granting the order bankrupting Goldstate.

As Bolton was leaving the court, Lossan caught up with him and told him that the RCMP had retained legal counsel and wanted to meet as soon as possible.

***

Bolton met with Lossan and the Crown lawyers the Mounties had retained the following afternoon at the lawyers' office across the street from the courthouse on Smithe and Hornby. The bank's lawyer didn't have much to say and spent the meeting leaning back in his chair with arms crossed. Lossan, on the other hand, brought coffees for everyone and greeted them with his usual hearty handshake. Then he stood at the front of the room and summed up the situation: George Koehle had committed criminal acts by transferring properties, but the RCMP needed more information to proceed with a case. The two lawyers nodded in unison.

Bolton took his cue. "I was at Goldstate this morning with a locksmith. All the records are gone. Filing cabinets empty. And there was rubbish all over the place. It was as if someone left in a hurry. Nothing was left but furniture."

Lossan pulled out a chair and took a seat, looking around the table intently. "Next step, we'll get warrants for the offices and residences of…" He looked down at some papers for a moment. "Here it is. Garry Steiner. The company's lawyer. And their accountant, Harry Choi. We'll also want to check out Koehle's residence."

"What are you looking for exactly?" Bolton asked.

Lossan shifted his huge body in the small chair. "Well, for starters, I'd like to find out if the gang was funding the business and using it for other purposes. Likely laundering. Koehle might've destroyed records, I doubt Choi did."

"You think he'll cooperate?"

"He's a chartered accountant. I doubt he'd risk his designation for someone like Koehle. And why would he destroy his own files? Besides it's hard to believe he's involved in this. Now, if he doesn't cooperate, that could suggest he's involved."

Chapter 6

Paul Bolton met Lossan in the lobby of the RCMP Commercial Crime headquarters on Heather Street at 7:00 a.m. on Friday. He'd never been involved in a raid before.

Lossan greeted him with a wide grin. "Nervous, Paul?"

"A little. I didn't sleep much last night."

"You'll be fine. People under investigation tend to cooperate. Choi won't be any different. He'll call his lawyer. His lawyer will ask to see the warrant, but at the end of the day, he'll have no choice. We'll find out how involved he is in George's little scheme and who knows what else. Having you along is a bonus. You know what to look for. You used to be an auditor, didn't you? You'll be able to tell if he's bullshitting us or not."

In Bolton's experience, most frauds were straightforward. He thought of the two schemes he'd come across at a car dealership up in Prince George. The dealer delayed reporting and paying for its new-car sales. This meant the dealer overstated its cash and car inventory. When the finance company attended the dealership to verify the new-car inventory, there would be cars missing from the lot. The dealer claimed they were at a different location or in transit or being sold on consignment, or they were cars that had been sold weeks before but the dates on the invoice changed. And the finance company never followed up on all the lame and bullshit excuses the dealer gave as to why the cars weren't on the lot.

As he dug deeper, Bolton discovered a cheque-kiting scheme. Every two weeks, the dealer would issue a cheque payable to a numbered company owned by the dealer and deposit it with another bank. A week later, the numbered company would pay the money back to the dealer. Relying on the fact that most cheques took between three to four days to clear, the dealer was able to report that they had a lot more cash on hand than they really had.

The car dealership had been trying to hide mounting losses for ages and the two frauds had been going on for years. When the dust settled, the auto finance company lost over two million dollars.

As Lossan pulled the transit van into the Broadway Avenue parking lot, they stopped at the entrance.

"How long will you be here?" the attendant in the booth asked.

"Give me a ticket for the whole day."

They parked the van in the loading bay, and Lossan pulled out a Police sign and put it on the dashboard. It was 7:50 a.m. The attendant tapped on the window. "Hey buddy, you can't park there!"

Lossan jumped out of the van, towering above the attendant, and pulled out his identification. The attendant backed off and headed back to his booth.

Lossan got back in the van, looked over at Bolton and smiled. "Time to visit Mr. Choi."

As they entered the lobby of the sixteen-storey building that had seen better days, they walked over to the office directory and looked for Choi's name. "Harry A. Choi & Associates, Chartered Accountants. Suite 1400."

Choi's firm had the whole floor. Lossan headed straight to reception. A young Asian woman sitting at reception asked if she could help them.

"We're here to see Mr. Choi please."

"Do you have an appointment Mister … sorry I didn't get your name?"

"It's Lossan, Pat Lossan."

"I'm very sorry, but Mr. Choi has meetings all morning. If you'd like to leave your business card, I'll let him know you popped by, and he'll be in touch very shortly."

Lossan gave her his card. Bolton admired Lossan's self-confidence. It reminded him of the time he'd applied to join the fraud squad, part of the Metropolitan Police in London. But the interview didn't go well. He'd been told that after the mandatory two years on the beat as a bobby, he'd be assigned to a particular division. When they mentioned Bomb Squad, he'd wavered. Looking back, he realized they were trying to find out if he was serious about joining the police. And he knew it wasn't for him. This, on the other hand, was fun.

In less than a minute, a short, balding Asian man came out of his office. "I'm Harry Choi, how can I help?"

"Hello, Mr. Choi. My name is Pat Lossan and I'm with the RCMP Commercial Crime Division. This is Paul Bolton from Kinsey & Company. It's about one of your clients. I wonder if we can meet somewhere more private?"

"Of course, please come into my office. Janis hold my calls."

Choi led the way to his large corner office, which had a spectacular view of downtown Vancouver. He motioned to the chairs in front of his desk.

"Gentlemen, what's this all about?"

"We're here about Goldstate Finance. We have a warrant to search your offices. We're looking for any records you have in connection with that company." Lossan handed Choi the warrant.

"I don't have any company records."

"We're here for all your audit working paper files, correspondence, bank statements and anything else to do with the company."

Choi started blinking and turned pale.

There was a knock on the door. "What is it?"

The receptionist quietly opened the door and said, "Mr. Choi, I'm sorry to disturb you, but the caller said it was urgent."

"Not now, take a message." Choi's face started to turn red.

"Mr. Choi, I really think you should take this call. It's your wife. The police are at your home."

Choi picked up the phone. He said something in what sounded like either Cantonese or Mandarin. He tried to cover the phone, but Bolton could hear a screaming high-pitched voice on the other end. Choi said something in a staccato voice and then hung up and turned to face the men in his office again. His face had lost its colour. "Would you give me a few minutes to call my lawyer?"

Twenty minutes later, Choi came out of his office and asked them to join him in the boardroom. Some of the colour had come back into his face. "Where do you want to start?"

"How about you bring us all your files on Goldstate," Lossan said.

"Certainly. If you give me a few hours, I can have everything put together and brought to the boardroom. Why don't you gentlemen go and have a coffee and come back at eleven."

Lossan smiled and took a step forward. "We're not going anywhere until we've had a chance to access your computer system. Your staff will have to stop work immediately. Why don't you tell *them* to go for a coffee?" There was a knock on the door. Lossan kept his eyes on Choi. "That'll probably be one of my guys."

A lanky, spectacled individual, about thirty, entered the room. Lossan glanced at him and then gestured. "Mr. Choi, this is Constable Eric Dyer from the RCMP Commercial Crime Division. He's going to go through your database and download all the files we need." Choi groaned.

Eric asked Choi to arrange for whoever was responsible for their IT to come in so he could ensure that no one accessed the system until he'd finished. He thought it shouldn't take more than two hours.

"So now would be a good time for your staff to go for that coffee," Lossan said. "Or, better yet, an early lunch. Say ... two hours?"

Choi threw up his hands. "Is all this really necessary?"

"I can assure you, it'll be easier for everyone this way. We'll be out of your hair as soon as possible." Bolton leaned closer to the RCMP officer and said something in his ear. Lossan nodded and looked back at Choi. "Now, who worked on the Goldstate audit?"

Choi sank into the chair behind his desk. "Darryl Yip, one of our managers, was in charge."

"Please ask him and your IT person to come in here before taking lunch, and we can get started. Then you can tell everyone else they can leave."

Choi sighed. "Do you have to be here when I speak to my staff?"

"No, but we will have to tell your IT administrator and Darryl Yip why we're here."

Ten minutes later, Eric had disappeared with the IT administrator, and Lossan and Bolton were meeting with Darryl Yip. Choi was in the room, but he didn't appear to be taking much in. Finally he got up and said, "Is it okay if I call my staff together and tell them what's going on now?"

As Choi left the room to meet his staff, Bolton wondered what the man was thinking and whether he knew about the property transfers.

"Well, you don't need me," Lossan said, heading out of the boardroom.

Bolton spent the next few hours reviewing files with Yip, who left the room once in a while to collect more information. On one of these occasions, Lossan walked back into the room. "How's it going, Paul?"

Bolton looked up from where he was sitting at the long table in the boardroom. Papers and file folders were strewn around him, and two half-empty coffee mugs were on one side. "Darryl doesn't seem to be holding anything back. He's given me files for the last three years. He's been on the audit for five years. Goldstate is one of their biggest clients."

"Does he have any idea about the property transfers?"

"If he does, he's not saying. And he seems as surprised as anyone about our visit."

Lossan shrugged. "All right. Well, I'm going to check in and see if anything turned up at Koehle's or the lawyer's residence. I'll check back later."

Bolton was talking to the RCMP constable who was looking at the company's computer system when Lossan returned to the boardroom an hour later. The firm had a basic accounting software system for preparing monthly financial statements for clients, but nothing in connection with Goldstate. Eric had printed a list of their clients—there were more than six hundred names. Most of them were numbered companies. But there was no information on Goldstate. The officer left.

Lossan pulled out a chair and sat at the table next to Bolton. "So, what do we know so far?"

Bolton leaned back in his chair and raised his hands together over his head and sighed. "I've looked at everything for the past three years. Most of what I saw is what you'd expect to see in an audit file. And, as is the practice, a lot of the material in the files was prepared by the company. As usual, the audit tick marks and other initials were made by Darryl or other members of the audit team. The monthly financial statements were prepared in house. And there were a lot of journal entries and year-end adjustments."

"Is that unusual?"

"Not really. It reflects on the quality of Koehle's accounting staff and the financial statements. More adjustments means the auditors had to correct more."

Lossan looked bored, as if he were expecting something more than a lesson in auditing. "So, that's it?"

Bolton picked up one of the coffee mugs, glanced into it and set it down again with a frown before looking up at Lossan again. "There's something you might want to look at."

Lossan grinned. "Cut the crap. What have you found?"

Bolton was enjoying himself. He thought back to his years in audit in London. He imagined himself in Darryl Yip's shoes and wondered what he would do if he were in charge of the audit. What sort of questions would he have asked, how skeptical would he have been? He thought back to the time when he was late for a company inventory count and made the company start the count all over again. He wasn't popular that day. Darryl Yip wasn't a by-the-book kind of auditor. He accepted everything he saw. It took a fairly strong personality to question things. Most of the audits he'd worked on could best be described as ticking boxes, asking the same questions as last year and definitely not thinking outside the box.

"Are you thinking about those threatening phone calls again?"

Bolton was slightly startled and looked up at Lossan again. "Huh? No. Just thinking about the process. And Davis." Bolton scrunched his forehead up. "I can't figure out how Davis fits in. Darryl said he dealt with several people at the company, but never Davis. Usually it was someone with an accountant or bookkeeper title and the payables and receivables clerk. He wasn't sure what Davis's role was at the company in the three years he'd been there, but he never filled the role of controller, or any other financial role for that matter. He'd never even met the guy. There'd been some turnover and the previous bookkeeper left suddenly and wasn't replaced. According to Darryl, the company wasn't ready for this year's audit and that's why it was late. Choi would always review the year-end financials with Koehle and Davis. Darryl Yip was never involved."

"What are you saying?" asked Lossan.

"If Davis was really a controller, he'd have been involved in the year-end audit, and Darryl would have dealt with him, especially since Darryl did most of the work. Davis was controller in name only. Or that was what George would like people to think he was anyway."

"That makes sense. So that's it?"

"Well, there's one thing that's bothering me. Look at this schedule of the company's year-end real estate property."

"What am I supposed to be looking for?"

"Beside each property are initials."

"And?"

"Well look at this." Bolton pulled one of the files toward him and flipped it open. "See for yourself. This is the list of names of the individual investors that makes up the investor debt schedule. If you compare the names with initials on the property schedule, they match up. And here is the list of investors and the property list with the initials beside each property."

Lossan looked a little lost. "What are you getting at?"

Bolton looked up at his friend. "Somebody used the property list as a record of which investor was to get which property and then wrote down the investors initials next to the property they were getting."

Lossan spent a few minutes cross-checking the list of properties with the investors' names.

Bolton explained. "I couldn't figure it out at first, but I noticed Choi's name on the office directory when we arrived this morning. His company was listed as Harry A. Choi & Associates. So, I looked for the initials H.A.C. and found it on the property list. Then I started to compare the others, and they all matched: G.S. for Garry Steiner, F.F. for Florence Fominoff, K.E.K. for Kevin. E. Kalishnikov, and so on. Here's my handwritten summary of the property transfers that Koehle made to the investors. They match up."

"But why would they leave it in the audit file?"

"I asked Darryl about it. He claims it's the first time he's seen the initials and he doesn't recognize the handwriting. Maybe it was Choi, maybe it was Steiner, maybe it was Koehle. My guess is it was most likely Koehle. Each property has a different value; maybe he was trying to match up the investor loan to the property value and use a copy of this schedule so that his lawyer, Steiner, would know which investors would get which properties when he prepared the property transfers. Who knows?"

Lossan smiled. "Hmmm… It's hard to believe it's that simple."

"I'm sure I'm right. I've double-checked both the US and Canadian property schedules with the investor list and they all match. There were a few investors that didn't receive properties and they don't show up on the property schedule. Look, here's my notepad where I listed the initials and compared them to the investors."

Lossan looked at his notepad and then stared at him. "Good work, my friend. Okay, is there anything else we need right now?"

"No, but we should take all these files with us."

Lossan stood up. "I'll get Choi."

Lossan returned with Choi and sat down next to Bolton, who was putting the files in boxes on the table. "We're just about done, Mr. Choi," Lossan said. "And as you can see, we're taking a few files with us. I'll make sure we give you a list of the files before we leave."

Bolton thought Choi looked like he had a bad bout of the flu. He seemed to have developed a greenish tinge over the past few hours. The short man pulled a handkerchief from his jacket pocket and patted his shiny forehead. "I hope you didn't waste your time today. I don't know what you expected to find."

Lossan crossed his arms and looked across at the other man. "Your firm could be the only source of information about the company's financial history."

Choi leaned back in his chair. "Why did you visit my residence?"

Lossan smiled. "Until we can determine exactly what's happened, we have to consider every possibility."

"You think I am part of this?" Choi's face regained some of its colour.

"Are you saying you knew nothing about the property transfers?"

The small man's lip trembled, though Bolton thought it looked more like fury than fear. Choi tucked his handkerchief back into his breast pocket and frowned. "I would like to cooperate, but my lawyer tells me that there is no requirement for me to answer any of your questions."

Lossan bit his lip and studied Choi for a few seconds, but he only said, "Here's a list of files we're taking with us."

Bolton sensed Choi was about to say something but then decided against it. They both thanked Choi, taking the boxes of files with them. A few minutes later, as Lossan pulled out of the parking lot, he asked Bolton what he thought of Choi.

"He's pissed. And scared. I'm not sure how involved he is, but he knew about the transfers."

Back at Heather Street, Lossan asked Bolton to join him while they called the officers who'd visited the other locations. They learned that Steiner's offices gave up just about nothing. They'd obtained copies of the company's BC real estate transfers showing that Steiner had acted as counsel, along with details of the lawyer's trust account and a history of his billings to Goldstate for the last twelve months. Steiner was livid that cops went to his home. His housekeeper let them in, but they didn't find anything other than some pornography hidden in the bottom draw of his office desk. Lossan smirked.

One of the Mounties who attended Choi's residence was fluent in Cantonese and had been there when Mrs. Choi called her husband at his office. He reported that she said something about Choi being stupid to get mixed up in this, Davis being a crook, and Koehle a fool. She then became guarded, said something he couldn't make out and hung up. The officers didn't find any records relating to the company but did find large denominations of both US and Hong Kong dollars and two dozen five-ounce gold bars.

The officers that visited the Koehle residence reported that they found Koehle's wife, Thelma, and son, Karl, at home. Karl had to be handcuffed and put in the back of the police cruiser because he refused them access and was shouting obscenities all the time, mostly about Paul Bolton. They didn't find any records or a computer or any sign of George. They were confident he wasn't in Hawaii since his passport was in his desk. His wife initially claimed she hadn't seen him in almost two weeks and didn't know where he was, and then she said he was in Hawaii.

Chapter 7

The weather had been bad for several days and there'd been daily snow flurries. It looked like it might be an early winter this year. Davis decided to put off the trip to the lodge until there was a break in the weather. By Friday, things finally improved, and he thought it'd be a good day for a drive.

As he'd done every day for the past week and a half, George awoke around 8:30 a.m., got dressed and headed to the kitchen for something to eat. And, as usual, he could see Davis through the window, sitting on the outdoor bench with a coffee.

About fifteen minutes later, Davis was back inside. "You eaten anything?" he asked.

George nodded.

"Good. We need be on the road soon."

George frowned. He didn't want to get in the car again. Quite frankly, he'd been happy staying in the cabin and reading books all day. And why did Davis insist on taking him to this lodge? "How far away is it?" George asked.

"Almost two hours. We should go now before it gets too late or the weather changes." Davis was already heading out the door.

George took a last slug of coffee and grabbed his coat. They were on the highway a little before nine. George wanted to ask Davis how long he'd be up here at the cabin, but he wasn't sure when the right time was. He'd tried broaching the subject earlier, but Davis had shut him down and only said he'd be up there for as long as necessary.

The lodge was about seventy-five kilometres west of Anahim Lake, but the conditions were good. It was sunny and dry, and there was little traffic. After a while, the highway began to climb. "This is pretty steep," George said.

"It climbs about six hundred metres until it reaches the Heckman Pass at the top of Bella Coola Hill. We'll be over fifteen hundred metres high there."

They got to the Heckman Pass after about thirty minutes and started going downhill again. George yawned. Then he noticed they were on a dirt road. What the heck! Then a road sign with bright orange borders and words across the top and bottom: STEEP GRADES AHEAD. BRAKES ADJUSTED? Within less than a kilometre they reached a hairpin, and the road turned back on itself. George gasped and grabbed his seat. A few kilometres farther down the hill, they started to navigate a tight S curve. George moved away from the side of the vehicle to get away from the cliff.

"Relax," Davis said, staring out the windshield.

"Maybe you should slow down a bit," George said. Davis didn't seem to notice.

George looked over to the left side of the road and down the steep hill. Apart from dense forest, all he could see were switchbacks going down and down the hill. The road went on forever.

A strange thought floated through George's mind and he felt suddenly very weak. *What if Davis isn't helping me? What if he wants to get rid of me? That might solve his problems. And this would be the perfect place.* George held onto his seat with both hands, his white face turned toward the window, his thoughts spiralling, his stomach feeling empty. *In the middle of nowhere, in a place full of grizzly bears. He could push me out of the vehicle over the side of the cliff or just stop by the side of the road, shoot me, and push my body down the mountain into a ravine. They'll find my body in the springtime, or what's left of it after all the wild animals have finished.*

George looked at Davis. He wanted to say something but was frozen by fear. He watched his every move, waiting for the vehicle to slow and stop. The engine growled as it geared down.

"How long before we get to the lodge?" George shouted.

"Twenty kilometres."

That's it, keep him talking, George thought. "Is the road like this all the way?"

"Pretty much."

A sign announced the start of the avalanche area. George closed his eyes. The Land Rover geared down again as the vehicle took another sharp bend, pulling him sharply over toward Davis. Most of the dirt road was one lane. George was often on the cliff side of the road with nothing separating him from a sheer thirty-metre drop. He looked out his window and could see another hairpin below.

"That's the Atnarko Glacier Road bridge. It's about three kilometres away," Davis said. They came to an area where you could pull over and look at the view. "Want to stop and take a look?"

"No." That was the last thing George wanted to do.

"We're almost at the lodge. You can stop holding that seat so tight."

George breathed a sigh of relief. The end of the hill. They passed a rest area. Two hundred metres farther down the hill and two switchbacks later, there was a sign for the lodge. They turned left off the road and followed the gravel drive.

"What did you think of the Hill?" Davis asked.

"I need a washroom."

"The lodge is closed, so it's either the bush or Bella Coola."

"The lodge is closed? Why did we even come here?" George's fears had brought out a prickly side. He was tired of being in the car and even more tired of being terrified. He felt sick and wished he'd never come up here with Davis. He would've been better off taking his chances with the police.

"You okay?" Davis asked.

George just looked out the window.

They drove around the lodge buildings and Davis stopped the car. "Do you want to get out and stretch your legs?"

"Let's keep going."

It was 11:30 a.m. by the time they pulled into the small fishing village of Bella Coola. They parked by the government wharf and walked past a place called the Float House Inn located by the dock. It was closed so they headed into the village. Davis pointed to a small restaurant on the main street. Inside there were about a dozen tables, but only one was occupied by a couple of older locals. Davis ordered the West Coast eggs benny. When the waitress looked at George, he shook his head. "I'm not hungry." He excused himself from the table and headed to the washroom. For a moment, he thought of trying to escape, but he where would he go? He returned to the table.

After Davis finished his meal, they headed out to explore the village on foot. Fishing season was over, and the place almost shut down. They walked up the street and passed a plaque commemorating the first white people who settled the area in 1894. Then they wandered back to the Land Rover.

"Last chance to eat something," Davis said.

"I'm fine."

George was quiet on the way back. He was confused. Davis had plenty of chances to get rid of him. But he actually seemed concerned about him. It didn't make sense.

They arrived back at the cabin around four. Davis cooked some late-season halibut that he'd picked up in Bella Coola and they both had a cold beer. They even played a few games of cribbage. When they were done, George picked up a couple of books from the bookshelf. One about the history of the area, the other about bears. He settled back into a chair and opened one of the books.

Davis took the bottle of blended whisky off the counter and carried it to the table with his mug. "We need to talk about Goldstate. Plan our next move," Davis said.

George stared at the words on the page of his book, taking in nothing. He looked up and found Davis staring at him. "Oh. That. Yeah, there's something I've be meaning to tell you…"

Davis tipped some whisky into his coffee and sat down again. "I'm listening."

"Well … I was worried about the investors after the bank called the loans and you said you—your boss, that is—wouldn't refinance the business. And well, you see, Davis, those investors are like family. Thelma … she would never forgive me if she found out. And my lawyer said … well, he said we should transfer the properties to the investors before the bank takes over."

Davis set an elbow on the table and glared at George. "You transferred the properties? This is *after* I told you to shut the place down."

George glanced away and swallowed. "Well, yes, I—"

"What did you think was going to happen when the bank found out?" Davis's mind was spinning. He'd planned to spend a few weeks up north, figure out a plan and then report to McVittie in Vancouver. Now he'd have to get back to the coast before the Mounties got involved and it all blew up. "And it's taken you all this time to tell me? Christ almighty, George, do you know what you've done?"

He pushed his chair back, grabbed his mug and the bottle of whisky and headed off to bed, ignoring George's feeble attempts to discuss the issue further. He needed to think. Davis shut the door to his room and lay on his bed still fully clothed, staring up at the pine boards on the ceiling. Once the bank found out about the transfers, there'd be a major investigation. They'd try to get the properties back. That meant going through the books. Getting the goddam Mounties involved. Sooner or later, they'd find out about the gang's involvement. And McVittie would not like that. Davis needed to make sure that any paper trail back to McVittie was well covered.

And that meant getting rid of George.

Davis turned his head and looked at the picture of his ex on the table. He sighed. There was no way he could contemplate leaving the gang now. He looked away from the picture. Was he really thinking about killing George? He sat up and took a sip of his whisky, dark thoughts on his mind. It would need to look like an accident, or better still, suicide. Unless they never found the body. Where could he hide a body for a long time? This place would've been perfect, but it was the wrong time of year. The ground was already frozen. He could hide it for the winter and then come back and bury it in the spring. As long as some wild animal didn't find it in the meantime. It'd be better to take care of him on the coast and easier to bury the body.

Davis grabbed the bottle of whisky. *What the hell am I thinking? Is this what I've become?* He poured the rest of the whisky into the empty coffee mug. There had to be another way. Maybe he could hide George, pretend he'd been dealt with, but that would require help. And even a few weeks up here would be a challenge for George. His mind circled back. No. He couldn't protect George and keep himself safe. The more he thought about it, the more he knew he wasn't dealing with the real issue. He couldn't separate his problem from George's. He needed to deal with him. If he didn't, the gang would, and then they'd likely deal with him as well. If he were McVittie, he'd be sending the boys up north right now. Find a way to make it look like the pair of them disappeared, find a remote spot in the bush where he could hide the bodies. But none of the gang were outdoorsmen, nor were they smart enough to plan something like this. And McVittie wasn't a planner. He reacted to events rather than controlled them. But if Davis didn't report to him soon, the boss would know something was wrong. And the longer he stalled, the more likely McVittie was to take matters into his own hands. He may already have.

Davis drained his mug and set it on the bedside table. If only he had the luxury of living in George's world. Here he was worrying about what he should do next, while George was probably sleeping like a baby.

***

George had not been able to read after Davis left the kitchen. He'd never seen the man so angry. And suddenly those earlier fears resurfaced. It would be easier for Davis if George were dead. George crept to his bedroom, shut the door quietly and wedged a chair against it. *At least if he comes for me in the night, I'll hear him. I'll have a chance.*

But no weapon, he realized. He looked out the window. It was pitch black. There wasn't even a moon. He couldn't fight, he couldn't escape. He was completely in Davis's control. He was trapped.

Sometime during that long night, George must have fallen asleep because he was startled awake at 7:30 a.m. by a sharp rapping.

"I'm leaving now," Davis called through the door.

George jumped out of bed, found a sweater and pushed his arms through it before opening his door. Davis was just heading outside.

"You're leaving?"

Davis stopped and turned around. "In case you haven't realized, we're in a goddam mess."

"You mean because of … but you're not staying?" George realized that meant Davis wasn't going to kill him. Not right away anyhow.

"I'm heading back to the coast. I'll be back before the end of the week. You just lie low."

"What if I run out of firewood?" George said, following him outside.

Davis pointed to the side without stopping. "There's an axe on the porch."

"What about a phone?" he asked.

"I never needed one."

Then he got into the Land Rover, reversed and tore out of the driveway without looking back.

Chapter 8

Karl Koehle had just got home after having a few beers with friends at a pub in Burnaby. Over the last few days, he'd been trying to figure out what had been going on in his dad's business. He knew he was a disappointment to his parents, especially his father. He wasn't good at school and couldn't wait to leave. He'd always liked messing around with cars and his dad had found him a job at a garage where he'd hoped to be a mechanic. Just like in school, Karl had trouble doing what he was told to do and didn't pay attention. When he started work at the garage, he was given menial jobs, like sweeping up and making coffee. He complained. Slowly, they started letting him do things like oil changes. But he was bored and kept complaining. One day, after one too many outbursts, the owner had had enough and fired him.

And that's how he ended up in the family business. For a brief moment, he made his father happy. George had always hoped that Karl would one day take over Goldstate. But it quickly became apparent that Karl didn't like being cooped up in an office, and worse, he really didn't understand the business. He wasn't good with numbers, and he didn't like being surrounded by all the women in the office who were always gossiping. He lost some documents once. Another time, he blabbed about some confidential information outside work. And because he was the boss's son, he was even less concerned about his behaviour at work than he had been at the garage. He was bossy with co-workers and sometimes rude to investors.

At the beginning, George had really tried to help him fit in. He'd taken Karl to important meetings with investors. One time, he let him sit in on a meeting with the bank. But it seemed the more Karl was exposed to, the less he understood. After a few months, George offered to send him to college part time to do some accounting courses, but Karl knew it wasn't for him. And in the end, his dad only kept him around because he had nothing else to do.

So, it wasn't surprising that the day Bolton had visited the office, Karl was there, albeit, sitting sullenly in the lunchroom, just off reception, reading a comic book with his feet up on a chair and a can of Coke next to him. He probably wouldn't have noticed Bolton at all if the receptionist hadn't been blathering on about the man to someone on the phone. Women were so easily taken in by an accent.

It was after that meeting that Karl began to notice the change in his dad. He seemed to shrink into himself somehow. His shoulders seemed more rounded and his step slower. Karl shrugged it off, but a few days later, when he heard his dad comment about the bank hiring Bolton to look at the company's books, he noticed a darker, almost desperate, tone.

Karl hadn't gone to the meeting the next day. But he heard people talking later. And he was a little annoyed that his dad didn't tell him in advance that the office would be shutting down. He didn't even know if he'd be getting paid. And now there were rumours that his mom was coming back to work once his dad got back from Hawaii. Karl thought it might be nice to go to Hawaii, and he was even more annoyed that his dad hadn't bothered to invite him. It would have been a good learning experience, after all. And the sunshine wouldn't hurt. But the more he thought about it, the more Karl wondered, if they were going to Hawaii to raise money, why shut down the office?

And this had been a last-minute thing. Didn't business trips take a bit of planning and cost money? The next day, when his father didn't call to tell them he'd arrived safely, Karl began to worry.

That night at home, he'd asked his mom, but she didn't know anything other than what his dad had told her—cash was tight, and they needed to raise some money. His mom told him things would be fine, but he could tell she was worried too. Whatever the mess his dad was in, it could finish him, especially after his bankruptcy years ago. Karl had been a little boy when his dad had needed to go away for a while. He remembered the kids at school telling him his dad was a loser and had mental problems. He later discovered that his dad had been in Riverview Mental Hospital. His parents never talked about those days. He knew now that his dad had tried to commit suicide.

Karl frowned. All their problems started after Bolton's visit. Karl needed to find out what happened in that meeting. If Bolton was the problem, he needed to find a way to stop him. That's why he'd made the phone calls. Maybe he could scare him off. Buy some time while he figured out what was going on. Karl thought about Alan Davis again. He seemed to be right in the middle of all this.

Davis had never spoken directly to him, and Karl was secretly a little scared of the man. He thought back to an evening a few months before when he was still at the office after everyone else had left. He'd wandered into his father's office and looked at the papers on his desk. There was a letter from the bank about overdue interest, some letters from investors complaining they'd not received any interest in months, and some draft financial statements that he couldn't understand. He'd sat in his dad's chair and opened the right-hand desk drawer and found a small bottle of Grand Marnier on top of a bunch of files. *The crafty old bugger*, he thought. At least Karl didn't hide his drinking, unlike his dad. He wondered if Mom knew. He pulled out the files. Most were monthly financial statements. At the bottom of the drawer was a small slip of folded paper. He opened it and recognized his dad's spiky handwriting. He could barely make out the word *Davis* and what looked like a phone number. Davis was mysterious and seemed important to his dad. Perhaps that's why he took one of his dad's business cards from the desk and wrote the number down on the back of the card and stuck it in his wallet. A guy like Davis could come in handy. Especially if his dad was in over his head.

Karl slid forward on the couch, pulled his wallet from his back pocket and looked through it until he found Davis's number. He thought about making a call but didn't. It was late. *Never make important decisions late at night.* His mother had said that many times. He headed down the hallway to his room. He'd sleep on it. And tomorrow, maybe he'd call, leave a message. When Davis got back from Hawaii, they could meet. If his dad wasn't going to give him answers, then maybe Davis would.

***

On the drive back to Vancouver, Davis thought again about leaving the gang. It was on his mind a lot lately. George was a complication he needed to deal with. What was he going to tell McVittie? Whatever it was, it had to be simple.

Davis was nothing if not methodical. He'd often agonize over the smallest detail and worry about things no normal person would even consider. And he knew that how he dealt with George would define who he'd become. Was he really going to kill him or help the gang get rid of him? Reluctantly, he admitted to himself that he actually cared about what people thought of him; not the McVitties of the world, but the daughter he hadn't seen in years, the ex-wife who'd left him. If he was serious about leaving the gang, he knew that the choice he made now about George's life would determine his future.

Davis arrived back in Vancouver around eight, after an uneventful drive. He didn't see anyone suspicious parked outside his home, but out of caution, he circled the block twice just to make sure. He'd seen enough cops staking out his place in the past to know what to look for. He knew he was being a bit paranoid, but that's how he survived.

He remembered one of the businessmen he'd read about years ago saying something about how only the paranoid survived. The guy ended up running a multi-million-dollar company. The guy was born in Hungary but escaped to the US after the Russians invaded his country. One of the guy's other sayings was "If you're wrong, you will die."

He opened the front door of his house and went straight to bed. He slept well for the first time in days.

***

At seven o'clock the next morning, the phone rang. Davis rolled over and pulled the receiver off its cradle. "Yeah?"

For a moment there was silence on the other end. Then somebody said, "Is this Davis? You're home. I thought you and my dad were in Hawaii."

It took Davis a minute to register what was happening. Then he sat up in bed. "Karl, right? George's kid?"

"Yeah. Where's my dad? Is he with you?"

"He's fine. He's lying low till this blows over." He was just about to hang up and go back to sleep.

"The police were at our house with a search warrant. They want to know where he is. Mom is going crazy. She's really scared. He's all right, isn't he?"

Davis sat up straighter. "Yeah, yeah, he's fine. Now tell me what happened."

"They were looking for the company's records and asking all sorts of questions about my dad, like where he is and when we saw him last."

"What did you say?"

"We didn't say anything. They couldn't find any records because my dad never kept any at home."

Davis breathed a sigh of relief. At least that was one less thing to worry about. "How long were they there for? Did your mom say anything?"

"About half an hour. Mom didn't tell them anything." Karl had to think about that since he'd spent most of the time in the back of a police cruiser and didn't want Davis to know. "She knows as much as I do. And hey, did you ever go to Hawaii?"

The kid was asking too many questions; it was as if he knew something. Davis needed to change the subject. "Have you heard from Steiner or Choi?" he asked.

"Who?"

"The company's lawyer and accountant. Listen, I'll call you back in a couple of hours." He hung up. Davis made himself a coffee and flipped open his Rolodex. He'd have to wait a few hours till their offices opened, but then he'd get some answers.

Steiner and Choi were both guarded on the phone, but they confirmed the police had raided their offices and their residences. Steiner said they hadn't found anything other than copies of the property transfers. The conversation with Choi was a little longer. The accountant said that they took a bunch of his files and asked lots of questions. They were particularly interested in the list of the company's properties and how the business had been funded. He said they were looking for bank statements, but they didn't have any. Choi thought it was strange, though, because it wouldn't take them long to get copies from the bank.

"How much do they know?" Davis asked.

"I think they were fishing. They brought a guy named Bolton with them. They shut down our office and accessed our computer system. They were looking for more than just Goldstate records."

"Whaddya mean?"

"They took our client list. Wanted to see if Goldstate had any other business interests. And they spent a lot of time on the property list. Then they took four boxes of files and left. I think they're going to try and reconstruct Goldstate's cash flow for the last few years."

Davis didn't think any of the seized records could be linked to the gang. The Reds never used Choi to do the books for any of their businesses, but the cops wouldn't know that. They were probably casting their net as wide as possible, hoping to catch something. But once they prepared a historic cash flow of the business, they'd discover all the money flowing in and out of Goldstate that came from companies owned by the gang. Sooner or later, they'd connect the dots. Even though they could be explained as business loans and it would be difficult to prove anything, that wouldn't stop the police. Under pressure, George might tell them that his company had been used as a cleaning house for the gang's cash. He didn't think that was likely, but...

Davis set his mug on the table. Who was he kidding? There was no telling what George would do and only one way to control him.

Davis had to tell his boss. Things were moving a lot quicker than he'd expected, and the last thing he wanted was McVittie hearing it from someone else. Sooner or later the police would start investigating the link to the gang. McVittie would blame him for the mess.

Davis showered and got dressed. He was making another cup of coffee when the phone rang again. Davis picked it up and heard Karl on the other end. "I've been waiting all morning. What's going on? Where's my dad?"

"Look, kid—"

"Tell me or I'm going to the police."

Davis closed his eyes. Another complication. He should probably make sure he didn't do anything stupid. "Mario's in an hour." He hung up.

**

Karl was already sitting at a table in the middle of the restaurant when Davis walked in. Karl raised a hand in greeting, but Davis just pointed to the back of the restaurant and walked past him. In a darkened corner, Davis sat in a booth with his back to the wall. A moment later, Karl sat opposite him, still holding his menu from the other table.

"So, where's my dad?"

"Keep your voice down." For 11:30 a.m. on a weekday, the place was already busy. "Your old man is fine. He's just keeping a low profile."

"My dad panics. He can't handle pressure."

"That's why I'm handling it. Only I know where he is, and it's staying that way."

Karl wanted to stand up and scream at this jerk. But he really didn't know Davis that well and he wasn't sure how he would react. So, instead, he just leaned forward and said in a low voice, "What about Bolton? Why don't we rough him up a bit?"

"We?" Karl thought he was going to see Davis smile for the first time ever. But the big man only gave his head a little shake and scratched the dark stubble on his cheek. "Bolton's not the problem. Threatening him will only make things worse. The bank's not going to back off."

"What are we—*you*—going to do then?"

Davis looked over Karl's shoulder and lifted his chin slightly, and Karl realized a waiter was standing beside him. "Whisky. Neat."

The waiter looked at Karl, his pencil poised above his pad.

Karl looked at Davis. "You buying?"

Davis muttered something under his breath, but before Karl could ask about it, the big man said, "Sure, kid. Order something."

Karl ordered a Peroni and was smart enough to wait for the waiter to leave before demanding Davis tell him more about his dad. Davis refused to say anything until the waiter had served their drinks. When they were alone again, Davis turned his attention back on Karl.

"You really wanna know what your dad's into?" Karl almost lost his nerve, but he nodded. "All right. A few years ago, your pop needed money quick. And he found some … people who would lend it to him, for a price. Not the sort that like to draw attention to themselves. You get me?"

Karl nodded.

"Well, your dad doesn't want to get on their wrong side, so he needed to disappear for a while."

"But couldn't we scare Bolton? Grab him outside his apartment building one morning and take him for a ride?"

Davis gritted his teeth. "I told you, Bolton's just the messenger. The bank won't let this drop. Now the goddam Mounties are involved."

Davis looked like he wanted to hit something, and Karl leaned back a bit. "But that's not who your dad has to worry about." He took a sip of his whisky and set the glass down. "The people your dad borrowed money from are dangerous. Once they discover the bank's called the loan and their money's at risk, they'll be looking for him."

Karl shrugged. "I still think—"

"You have no idea of the kind of people they are." Davis's dark eyes met Karl's small, green ones, and the younger man couldn't help glancing away. "Now, I'll keep you posted about your dad, but the less you know, the better. These people will come looking for him. And when they can't find him, they're gonna come talk to you." Karl looked up from his drink, his face a little paler than usual.

Davis tossed a couple of bills on the table, slugged back the rest of his whisky and slid out of the booth. "I'll call you when I know more."

When the waiter returned, Karl ordered a pizza and another Peroni. He peeled the label off the empty bottle as he thought back to the first time he'd seen Davis. It was a few years ago, back when his dad's business was first having problems. Then everything was fine for a while. And then Davis appeared. Karl hardly ever saw him at the office, and it was weird when he did. The way the guy looked—those scars, the creepy tattoo he saw once when Davis's sleeve was rolled up—not to mention the way he acted like he was the boss and Karl's dad was the one doing what he was told...

Karl took another bite of his pizza and chewed thoughtfully. If Davis wasn't going to do anything, maybe he should. Maybe now it was time for a face-to-face chat with Paul Bolton. The guy wouldn't be hard to take. And punching that pretty-boy face would be satisfying. Karl smiled. Yeah, a little chat with Bolton might be just the thing.

Chapter 9

At noon, Davis went to meet McVittie at the clubhouse. It was time to explain what had happened.

Davis's boss was a mountain of a man, but most of his muscle had turned to fat years ago. Leaning back in his chair, he squinted his small, dark eyes and scowled at Davis. "Let me get this straight: the police have records that link us to the company?"

Davis held his ground. "Boss, they won't get far with the records."

McVittie slammed a huge fist on the table. "Jesus Christ, Davis. How the fuck did you let it get this far? First you let this bastard transfer his assets to a bunch of bible thumpers, then he stiffs us for God knows how much money, and to cap it off, he's brought the cops to our door. That son of a bitch could take us all down."

"He won't. He can't."

"What the fuck does that mean?"

"He doesn't know anything. He thinks we're a bunch of loan sharks."

"He knows enough!" McVittie looked like a bull about to charge. "I gave you free rein, I let you run the whole show, but you've been sloppy, and you screwed up. Those bastards at the bank, they're not gonna let this go. And now the pigs are involved. And you know what? They don't give a rat's ass about the money. They want me."

Davis knew that reasoning with McVittie was hopeless, and he had to convince him that he'd given it a lot of thought and had a plan. He explained that all the bank statements would show were loans to the company from legitimate businesses. The loans got repaid on a regular basis. He'd made sure they appeared as arm's-length transactions, with interest charged and paid on a monthly basis. They'd have a hard time proving anything else.

McVittie's mouth drew into a tight line before he exploded. "Don't baffle me with bullshit! The fucking pigs will be all over this. Whether Koehle knows anything or not, they're gonna shine a light up our arse. I don't care if he knows nothing at all, get rid of him now. Do you hear me?"

"Yeah, boss."

"If you fuck this up, it won't be just Koehle that disappears. Understand?" McVittie stood up, walked over to him and looked down. "Damn right you do."

Davis didn't say anything. When McVittie got pissed, you just had to let him vent. There was no point in arguing with him; he never listened to reason.

"You clearly can't control Koehle, otherwise you'd have prevented him from transferring those goddam assets." Spit was flying from his boss's mouth now, and it was all Davis could do to hold his ground as he clenched his fists. "This is your goddam fault, Davis, and you need to fix it. Now."

Davis's jaw was clenched so tight it had begun to ache. He nodded.

"Where is the little bastard?"

"In a cabin, up in the Chilcotins."

"Good. Get back up there and take care of it." McVittie looked him in the eye, his head tilted slightly. "Why haven't you done it already?"

Davis almost groaned. This was exactly what he didn't want to explain. "I thought it would be best for things to die down, which they would have with Koehle out of the way. And I figured, we might need him. He didn't tell me about transferring the properties. What else is he hiding?"

McVittie rubbed his chin thoughtfully, his eyes drilling into Davis's.

Davis shifted slightly, then caught himself. He didn't want to appear nervous. "It needs to be done quiet like and—"

"What is this bullshit? You goin' soft? Get your ass up there and get rid of Koehle."

"But, boss, it won't take the Mounties long to figure out I had a place there and pin it on me."

McVittie almost smiled. "Only if they find a body." He leaned back in his chair. "I'll get a couple of the boys to go along with you. We don't want you having second thoughts, do we?"

He's going to get rid of me at the same time. Davis wiped his hand on his pants and hoped McVittie didn't notice he was fidgeting. He started to tell him that the ground was frozen up north at this time of year and he'd be lucky to dig a six-inch hole. A goddam bear or other animal would dig the body up before winter, and they'd come knocking on his door. "I need to get rid of him and leave no trace. No body, nothing. That'll take some planning. I'll drive him down to the coast, get rid of him somewhere out in the valley. Boss, the less you know, the better. My mistake, my problem. I'll fix it."

"And that kid you were telling me about? The one who keeps asking questions."

"I'll tell him I got his dad out of the country. I'll have George make a call. Make it sound real. Then I'll take care of it." Davis swallowed. There was no way out of this. Karl and his mother would think George was safe when what was left of him would be buried on some farm up the road.

McVittie looked him in the eye again. He let out a long slow breath and scratched at his stubble. "All right. Take him down to the coast. I don't wanna know where."

Davis nodded. "I'll use a couple of the boys, call them last minute. Boss, we don't want this coming back on you."

McVittie was still staring at him, and Davis could almost hear him wondering, *Does he have the balls? Is he really a killer?*

As Davis drove out of the yard, he knew McVittie figured he'd gone soft and that maybe he'd have to deal with him. He'd give him a day or two to get it done, and if he didn't, there'd be two bodies. He might even get one of the boys to follow him and find out exactly where he was hiding George.

Unless Davis dealt with George, his days were numbered. But if he planned on leaving the gang, murdering George just made it harder. Suddenly, all the dark thoughts he'd had for years seemed to plague him. If it weren't for Davis, McVittie would still be struggling to make a living. The man was a dumb, arrogant slob. Davis gritted his teeth. There was no other option.

He needed to get out.

***

Davis always kept a bag packed in his vehicle, so it was easy to head back to Anahim Lake instead of going back to his house again. He didn't want to risk having some of the gang follow him. With a bit of luck, he'd be there before midnight. It would give him time to think. He kept checking his rear-view mirror. Once it went dark, it was tough to tell. He stopped a few times on the way, but he didn't think he'd been followed. In all these years, the cabin was the one place that was all his. He'd never told anyone about it, but he knew McVittie would be able to find him. He'd have to move fast.

Davis thought about the plan and realized dealing with George in Anahim Lake would have been a mistake. The body might not have been found for ages, but sooner or later the Mounties would have brought him in for questioning. They'd get his vehicle licence number and would check video footage of traffic on the Trans-Canada Highway and Highway 97. They might even have footage of him and George in his vehicle. A title search would have shown him as the owner of the cabin. The Mounties would search it and find

George's fingerprints. No matter where he buried the body, they would eventually find it.

When Davis pulled up to the cabin, it was gone midnight, but the lights were still on. He wondered if George had found any of the weapons he'd hidden in the barn. If he'd been George, he'd have searched every inch of the place by now. He'd have figured out an exit strategy and armed himself as best he could, just in case the visitors weren't friendly. But he wasn't George—he trusted no one, left nothing to chance, always assumed the worst in everyone and everything. That was how he survived.

The cabin door was unlocked, and George was snoring in one of the chairs. Davis kicked his feet. George woke with a start. He looked as if he hadn't slept in a week.

"Bad news. The Mounties raided your home. They also raided Choi's and Steiner's offices and homes."

"What are they looking for?"

"Records."

"They won't find anything at my place."

"They took Choi's files. And they were looking for bank statements. What do they actually know, George?"

"Steiner doesn't know anything."

"What about Choi? Didn't he wonder about all the money going through the business?"

"He didn't care, as long as we paid his bills." George looked shaken. "They're going to find out I took a loan from your g—" He stopped himself and went pale. "From McVittie. I'll go to jail if they connect me to your boss … What are we going to do?"

"I'm going to get some sleep; we'll talk in the morning."

The last twenty-four hours had crystallized Davis's thoughts. It was decision time. Not only did he have to decide what to do with George, but whatever he did, he'd have to come up with a plan quickly. Was he overanalyzing the situation? Or was he just afraid of the decision he'd have to make.

Chapter 10

It was early morning. A red Mustang was parked outside Bolton's West End apartment building. The driver had been sitting in his car since 6:00 a.m., and it was getting light when Bolton and a young woman appeared at the front door of the apartment building. He kissed her and waved as she walked down the steps. The woman walked west along Alberni, and Bolton went back inside his building.

Karl Koehle started his engine, did a U-turn in the street and pulled the car up alongside the woman. She glanced at him over her shoulder and picked up her pace. Karl floored the gas pedal and caught up with her. He slammed on the brakes. He thought about getting out. But what would he say? And he didn't want her to see his face. He looked around and there was no one there. He then slammed the car back into gear and drove onto the sidewalk. The woman jumped at the noise, tripped and fell forward. Karl slammed the brakes again, pulled onto the road, did a U-turn and sped off.

***

Bolton's intercom buzzed and a moment later, perplexed, he let his girlfriend back into the building. Terry looked pale. Her knee was cut, and she was nursing her right arm. Bolton ran toward her. "My god, Terry, what happened?" If she answered, it was muffled into his shoulder, and he realized he wasn't going to get more at that point. He hugged her for a moment and then guided her into his apartment.

"Here, sit down." She wiped some mascara from her blue eyes and gulped a few times. Bolton noticed her left cheek was scratched. He went to the sink to fill a glass with water.

Terry took a long drink and couldn't seem to speak.

"It's okay. You're safe now," Bolton said.

She dried her eyes with a tissue. "Someone … just tried to … run me down."

She drank again, and the colour started to come back to her cheeks. "He was following me in his car and—and then I heard the tires … he drove up on the sidewalk. And I—I jumped out of the way."

"Is he still down there?"

She shook her head. "He drove away."

Bolton sat next to her on the couch and put his arm around her. She told him that she didn't get a good look at the driver. Bolton's mind was racing. He thought about the phone calls he'd gotten in the middle of the night. He thought about the dangerous people involved in this bloody case. About the gang. And Alan Davis. *What have I done? Have I put her in harm's way?*

Bolton thought back to the time he'd first met Terry. He'd been living in Vancouver for almost three years. Leaving London, his plan had been to travel. As a chartered accountant for one of the big international firms, transferring overseas had been easy. It wasn't everyone's choice, in terms of career advancement, but at thirty-one, with no real ties, he was looking forward to seeing more of the world.

A small city of about four hundred thousand people, you could drive across town in twenty minutes. Bolton settled in the West End just off Robson and Jervis. You could ski on the nearby Grouse Mountain and play tennis in Stanley Park the same day. The thousand-acre park was surrounded on three sides by the Pacific Ocean, and he never grew tired of walking there, even in the rain. He played tennis there too, and often had a beer on the deck of the Vancouver Rowing Club while enjoying the view of downtown from the water's edge. He even visited the zoo from time to time. That's where he met Terry. He'd been watching the chimpanzees and had started mimicking their behaviour, jumping from one leg to the other, using his hand to scratch under his armpit and making a funny noise, when he realized that someone was watching him.

"Do you recognize one of your relatives?"

He turned around and there she was. Freckled, with big blue eyes and straight brown hair that hung past her shoulders. He was embarrassed but quickly recovered. "More likely they recognize one of theirs."

She laughed. "I'm sorry, but you seemed to be having so much fun. It's good to see someone laugh at themselves."

He blushed. But she'd agreed to go out for coffee. They started dating soon after and spent many weekends wandering through the park together, enjoying the beautiful mountain and ocean backdrop. He didn't miss the London commute, the traffic, the masses of people or the noise. He did miss the Sunday papers and the pubs. But for someone who liked the outdoors, it was heaven. He'd read that people from BC were the healthiest in Canada. The air in Vancouver smelled cleaner and fresher. Everything was new. He'd travelled a lot as a young man and was used to being homesick. Settling in had been tough at first. It wasn't the friendliest place. It was old money, establishment. If you hadn't lived there for thirty years, you were an outsider. But Terry changed all that. She explored the city with him. And together they fell in love with it and each other.

But something else about the city caught his eye. Its dark side. Every city has one. And that was what he thought of now, as he held his girlfriend in his arms. Years ago, he'd seen some show about the port. About organized crime and the importation of illegal drugs. Port employees weren't subject to police background checks, and most of them got a job through a family member that worked there. Supposedly, many had criminal records and were open to bribes and not averse to redirecting shipments of anything from drugs to whole containers of high-end automobiles, specialized machinery and equipment, and illegal weapons.

The last three years flashed before his eyes. He thought about the threatening phone calls. About what happened to Terry today. And what could happen tomorrow. And he wondered if any of this was connected to George Koehle and this file he was working on.

Chapter 11

It was only 6:30 a.m., but George could hear Davis moving around in the kitchen. George rolled over. He didn't want to get up yet. He'd been doing a lot of thinking up north. The more he reflected on things, the more he realized he'd been used by the gang. At first, he'd needed them. Their money, specifically, and they were happy to lend it. When the market didn't improve, he should have sold some of his properties. But he just kept taking money from the gang. And as the loans increased, Davis spent more time at the company.

George frowned. He'd never questioned anything, partly because Davis scared him. Occasionally George caught bits of the big man's phone conversations. They often sounded threatening. Once Davis came in with a briefcase full of cash. Another time George overheard Davis having an argument with someone about shutting a place down. Later, when the amounts the gang put through the business got larger, George asked Davis where the money was coming from. Davis told him it was better that he didn't know. George thought the cash might be from the sale of drugs. Not that it made any difference, he could hardly tell them to stop. And then Davis told George he would be an owner of one of the gang's companies. He said it was a sign of confidence and trust in him.

Now George realized this was their plan all along. He was their insurance policy. He'd become a pawn in their business. Part of their business. One of them.

George had avoided talking to his wife about any of this. He wanted to, but he knew Thelma would be furious that he'd let it get this far. And he was never good at sharing problems with her. Now he was out of time. After everything she'd done for him, now he was going to lose her. And his family—the only thing that kept him going, the one constant in his life.

George got out of bed and shuffled into the kitchen where Davis was making coffee. "Little early, isn't it?"

Davis poured some coffee in a mug and handed it to George. "It's not safe to stay here any longer; the boys may be looking for you. And if they're looking for you, they'll be looking for me, too, and the Mounties may not be too far behind. We need to head back to the coast."

"You mean back home?" Several things flashed through George's mind. He'd have to face Thelma. He'd get to see his family again. And if Davis wanted to kill him, he'd probably do it here, not take him home again.

"We can talk about that on the way back. Pack up."

They left the cabin just before 8:00 a.m. The drive would take ten and a half hours without stops. Once they reached Williams Lake it was mostly highway, but it took nearly five hours to make the drive to Williams Lake on the Bella Coola single-lane road. Allowing for two stops on the way and for the traffic once they got to Hope, they should be in Vancouver before 9:00 p.m.

George started to feel better on the way back. He was almost cheerful. He knew he was an easy target up north, far from anywhere and without access to a phone. And it sounded like Davis was concerned that the gang may be looking for him as well. While he didn't completely trust Davis, he'd seen a different side of him up north. For all his tough exterior, he seemed to care. Maybe he was telling the truth. Maybe he would keep him safe.

Still, part of him couldn't help thinking about escaping at some point. He wondered, *What would Davis do?* He'd wait until he was out of the Chilcotins and closer to the lower mainland. He'd have thought it all through and developed a plan. Even a backup plan. George grimaced. He knew he wasn't Davis; he trusted people and never thought too far ahead.

A few hours later, thoughts of escape were still fuzzy. And anyway, it made no sense to try on the way back to the coast. All he'd seen along the way were forests and rugged mountains. The gas station they'd stopped at reminded him of a scene from the movie *Deliverance*. Even the guy pumping the gas scared him. Besides, this was Davis's backyard. Each time they stopped, he felt Davis's eyes on him.

A mountain man might have a chance escaping, George thought. *Hiding and surviving in such a place.* But not an out-of-shape city slicker whose only outdoor adventure was camping with his five-year-old son in the KOA campground in Surrey for two nights more than twenty years ago. Even then Thelma had visited them both nights and cooked for them. George sighed. If Davis hadn't been so intent on the road and in his own thoughts, he might have noticed.

Over a late lunch in a small town called Hope, Davis explained his plan. He'd booked a private plane to Costa Rica, where they'd both be going until things had blown over. They'd meet up with some friends of his that had a place there. George would be safe. They'd take care of him. And once he got settled down there, George's wife could visit.

George couldn't tell if Davis was serious, and he was shocked at the thought of leaving the country. One or two weeks he could understand. But when Davis told him his wife and son could visit once he was settled, he knew he was talking about months, if not years. Who knew what could happen to him down in Costa Rica. If that was the arrangement. Why, he may never come back. And was that the real destination? Or just an excuse to get him on a plane? Was there a plane? Spending time with Davis was rubbing off on him.

He looked out the window of the diner, watching the locals walking by and a guy filling up his car with gas. The name of the town made George laugh. Here he was in a town called Hope, having a meal with someone who was probably going to kill him. Hope was where they filmed the Sylvester Stallone movie *First Blood*. He remembered it was about a Vietnam vet arrested by police in a small town in rural Kentucky for some minor offence. The vet escapes and survives in the bush for weeks, pursued by police and state troopers. It had put the town on the map and provided jobs for a bunch of locals.

"What's so funny?" Davis asked.

"This town, it's called Hope." He sighed. "Your plan to fly down to Costa Rica … I'm not sure … it's a heck of a lot to take in."

"As I see it, we got two problems. The first is the friggin' Mounties, and what you'll say to them. They're going to want to know about our involvement."

"I was just trying to protect the investors from the bank, you know."

"Yeah. But that's called fraud, which means prison. You ever been to prison? I have, and you wouldn't last a week." Davis took a sip of his coffee and set it down again. "The second problem is the gang."

"I'll pay the money back, I swear it."

Davis looked very tired. "With what?" He shook his head. "Anyway, it's not about the money, it's about your silence. The gang doesn't want you talking to the Mounties."

"Why would I squeal?"

"Because if you're going down, you could take them with you." Davis set his fork down. "It's simple. They want you gone. If I don't get rid of you, they will, and then they'll take care of me too. That's how they operate. You get me?"

George turned pale. "Why are you telling me this?"

Davis hesitated. "I've … never killed anyone." He looked up for a reaction, but George's face was blank. "If I kill you, they'll have this over me. And I'm more concerned about them than the Mounties. You should be too."

George felt sick, but also strangely relieved. He sensed Davis wouldn't talk to him about this if he intended to kill him. Maybe there was another way to get out of this. "What if we just call the police right now and tell them everything?"

"Don't be an ass; we'd both be dead in a week."

"We could go into witness protection—"

"There is no protection from McVittie. Not in Canada. He'll find you. That's what he does."

George looked out the window and blinked a few times. His world felt very small all of a sudden. "Why Costa Rica? It seems so far—"

"Because the Mounties can't touch us there—if they do find us. Costa Rica doesn't have an extradition treaty with Canada. We go there first, then we talk to the police. In return for handing them the gang, we negotiate a deal, new identity, immunity from prosecution."

"How do I know I can trust you?" George realized it was a dumb question as soon as he opened his mouth.

"You don't," Davis said. "But if I wanted to kill you, you'd be dead by now."

George stared out the car window as they drove away from the diner. He didn't know whether it was sitting over lunch, casually discussing disappearing to another country, or the realization that there really were people who wanted him dead, but he knew his life was changed forever. He wondered if Davis had a chance of getting out of this mess and making peace with the gang. And he realized that without Davis, he had no way out. He'd have to trust him.

A few hours later, as they pulled off the highway heading into the city, Davis looked across and said, "It's time to say goodbye."

"What do you mean?"

"You need to tell your family you're going away."

"For a moment I thought you meant…"

"Christ, George, I told you I'm not going to kill you."

George settled back into this seat and looked out the window. "When?"

"Tomorrow."

He turned toward Davis again. "I need more time. My wife—"

"Your place isn't safe. The gang could soon be looking for both of us, and the police won't be far behind. We don't have any more time."

***

Paul Bolton and Pat Lossan were in one of the meeting rooms of the Mounties' Heather Street offices, briefing Lossan's boss, Inspector Hatley. They told Hatley that it looked as if George Koehle had panicked when the bank called the company loans and transferred all the real estate to his investors. The fact that the company lawyer and accountant received property, and the lawyer had notarized the transfer documents, showed that they had knowledge of the plan. It was unclear whose plan it was, but they didn't think Davis knew about it. This would be the last thing Davis would have wanted, since it would have resulted in the bankruptcy of the company and risked the trustee getting the Mounties involved.

Bolton had obtained statements from the bank for the last twelve months and estimated that over thirty million dollars flowed in and out of Goldstate's bank accounts from five different companies. Corporate searches revealed the registered owners were related to members of Davis's gang. Older bank statements showed deposits and withdrawals from the same companies going back two more years, but the dollar amounts were smaller. The transactions stopped around the time the bank's consultant met with Koehle and Davis.

Bolton took a deep breath after the lengthy explanation. He was having a hard time keeping his mind on this after what had happened at his apartment that morning. "I believe that Koehle's company was in trouble and he needed money. He ended up getting in too deep, and the gang figured it'd be a good front for laundering money. He probably didn't have a choice."

Hatley appeared doubtful and looked at Lossan. "Where do Steiner and Choi fit in?"

"Well, sir, there's nothing we've seen so far to suggest that Steiner or Choi had connections with the gang, but it's worth checking," Lossan replied.

Hatley wasn't satisfied. "Why would Davis allow the transfers? It doesn't make sense."

They were both looking at Bolton for some explanation, and it took him a moment to refocus. "Unless he didn't know," Bolton said. "The company's been losing money for some time, was poorly capitalized and had a lot of debt. Koehle may have asked them to put in more money and they said no. He panicked and didn't tell Davis."

Hatley looked at Lossan. "Does Koehle have a record?"

"No convictions, sir, but the superintendent of financial institutions investigated him ten years ago for transferring a property and mortgaging it without the clients' consent. The investigation was abandoned when the complainant failed to show up for the hearing."

Hatley leaned back in his chair and stared at Lossan. "We need to look further into this company and find out how the gang were involved. We should coordinate with RCMP Security Service." Lossan nodded. The Security Service had several ongoing investigations into local gangs. They were in regular contact with Criminal Intelligence Service Canada, who coordinated information sharing across the country between Border Services, the Mounties, Sûreté du Québec, the military, and provincial and city police forces. They probably knew all about Alan Davis. "Pursuing a criminal fraud investigation against George Koehle doesn't make a lot of sense on its own," Hatley continued, "but the gang, that's a different story. Establishing a money trail won't be enough. We need someone to explain the extent of the gang's involvement. Who knows, this may go a lot deeper than it appears at first glance." Hatley closed the file on his desk. "Find Koehle before the gang does and get him to talk."

"What if they already have him?" Bolton said.

"Then we're too late, Mr. Bolton. Pat, I'll call Security Service and get things moving." Hatley stood up. "Thanks, gentlemen. That's all for now," he said, then left.

Bolton gathered up his files and turned for the door as well, but found his friend standing in the way. "You want to tell me what's going on? You seem pretty distracted."

Bolton sighed. "Something happened. Just this morning, actually, and it scared the hell out of me."

Lossan lost his smile. "Another call?"

Bolton shook his head. It was hard to put his fear into words, so he just related the incident with Terry and the car in a matter-of-fact way. When he stopped talking, Lossan was frowning.

"She doesn't remember the make or model?" he asked.

"Just that it was red. It all happened so fast. And she was scared."

"Listen, Paul—"

"Actually, mate. I'd rather focus on work." Bolton was clutching the files to his chest, his face set with determination.

Lossan nodded. "All right. Let's get these bastards."

Chapter 12

Davis knew that taking George home was a risk. The gang could be watching the place, so could the police. They could even be watching his place. Was his paranoia kicking in? He doubted that McVittie would have acted so quickly. And he didn't think the police would commit resources to watch George's residence at this stage. But he knew that it wouldn't be long before the police and the gang would both start a manhunt.

He could easily have told George to get someone to bring his passport to him. But he wasn't ready yet, and besides, he really didn't care. Davis was going to leave no matter what. If George wasn't there tomorrow when he came back, he'd tell the gang about his plan to fly him out of the country and that George had changed his mind at the last minute. Alternatively, he could just forget about George and, sooner or later, the gang would deal with him.

Davis pulled into the small driveway of George's home and stopped the vehicle. "I'll be back tomorrow at two. Be ready, and remember, just a small bag and your passport."

"What about—"

"No more questions. You come with me or you take your chances with the gang."

George hesitated with his hand on the door handle. "What do I tell my wife?"

"Tell her you've met some people and will be gone for a while."

"Yes, but what about—"

"Keep it simple. The fewer people that know, the better. Remember, if you're not here tomorrow, you're on your own."

***

Thelma rushed to greet George as he walked in the front door, threw her arms around him and hugged him tightly. "The police were here. They said you didn't go to Hawaii. They found your passport. Where've you been? What's going on? Are you all right?"

"I'm fine, dear, I'm fine. Let me just come in and sit down. I'll tell you everything."

Hearing the front door open, Karl came down the stairs and hugged his dad.

"Where on earth have you been? Who was that in the driveway?" asked Thelma.

"Davis dropped me off. I've been … out of town."

"We've been worried sick. Why wouldn't you tell us where you were? What's going on?"

"Let me sit down first. How about a cup of tea, dear. I've been cooped up in a car for the last ten hours."

"Ten hours?"

"Please, Thelma." George sat down in his favourite chair and closed his eyes. He sensed Thelma walk away and then heard her in the kitchen. When he opened his eyes, Karl was staring at him. George looked down. What could he tell his son? A few minutes later, Thelma brought in a pot of tea and three cups. They were silent as she poured. And then George ran out of time. They were both waiting for an explanation. He took a sip of tea and set his cup down, then he told his family where he'd been and what Davis had planned. He described the plan to get out of town as nothing more than a precaution until things died down.

Karl remained silent, didn't make eye contact with his dad. But Thelma stared at him. She knew he wasn't telling them everything, probably torn between telling the truth about their lives being in danger and just skating over things. Ashamed that he'd screwed up again, she knew he was taking the easy option again. George never changed, more lies. Did he really think she believed that Davis, out of the goodness of his heart, took him all the way up to some place called Anahim Lake, in the middle of nowhere, so he could figure out a plan to hide him from the police? He'd never even told her about the company's problems with the investors, leaving her to hear from friends at church about the missed dividend payments. It was always the same. He never shared his problems; she always heard about them from someone else.

Thelma was a small woman, and not the type you'd notice when you walked into a room, but when she stood up and glared down at George, she had the complete attention of both men. "We've been married for thirty-three years, and in all that time I never questioned what you did. So, I want the truth. Tell me this instant what's going on, or you can take your bag and leave right now!"

George stared into her glossy brown eyes and felt his heart contract. He'd driven her to this. He looked down at his hands. "I told you the truth."

Thelma's lip quivered, but she settled herself with a slow breath. "Karl, please tell your dad to leave."

Karl had never seen his mom like this before. She even scared him. He looked at his dad. "Please, Dad, tell us what's going on."

George looked between them and then up at the ceiling. "I can't." He blinked a few times and looked out the window, beyond them both. And then in a quieter voice, he said, "Don't you understand? I don't want to drag you guys into this mess."

"You admit you're in trouble," said Thelma. She lowered herself slowly back into her armchair. "If you can't talk to us, how come you can talk to Davis? You trust him, but you don't trust us? Who are you really afraid of?"

"Thelma, if I tell you what's going on, then I put both your lives at risk."

They stared at each other across more than thirty years, and her face softened a bit. "Karl, can you give your dad and I a few minutes alone?" She stood up with her son and walked him out of the room, whispering something to him.

Karl nodded to his mom and then turned back toward his dad. "I'll just go to the store. I'll be back in twenty. Please tell Mom what's going on. We just want to help." Then he left, and Thelma returned to her chair looking determined.

"Go on, George," she said.

"Things aren't as simple as they appear," George said.

"They never are with you. But we can't help if we don't know what's going on. What's the worst that can happen?"

George looked down at the carpet. This was his way of dealing with things. Don't ask for help, try and sort things out on his own and shut down. When he looked up again, she was waiting. She'd seen that look on his face once before. He was scared, really scared.

"You and Karl mean everything to me," he said. "I want to protect you."

"Who from?" George shook his head, and she gritted her teeth. "How can you protect us if you're not here?" she asked. When he didn't answer, she pursed her lips and stood up again. "You lied to us about Hawaii, you're lying to us now. You were never a very good liar, you know. Where's he taking you?"

"I can't tell you."

Thelma walked over to the desk, pulled out his passport and waved it at him. "You won't be needing this then."

"You don't know what you're doing, just give me the passport."

"So, you *are* going out of the country this time?"

They stared at each other for a few seconds, and then George threw his hands up in the air. "Fine! Yes, we're leaving the country."

"And you trust this … Davis man?" She tilted her head a bit. "Who does he work for, George?" She knew instantly that he was going to lie. So, before he had the chance, she said, "Loan sharks?"

He shook his head.

"What's worse than loan sharks?" She was unsure whether to keep pushing him or wait and hope that he started to talk.

George took advantage of the silence. "All I know is that if I go to the police, I'll end up in prison, and I wouldn't last a week. The people I've been doing business with would … make an example of me."

Thelma turned pale, but she returned to her chair and sat, still holding the passport. "One last chance, who are they?"

George looked into his wife's eyes. She looked so tired. "Okay, okay. Look, I'm scared, I won't lie. The people I've borrowed from, well they're … bad people." George leaned forward and took her hands in his. She didn't resist. "Now the police are involved. Davis thinks … these *people* want to make sure that I don't say anything about them."

"What would you say?"

"Nothing! I don't know anything about their business, do I?" George realized he was gripping her hands tightly and loosened his fingers. In a gentler voice he said, "Davis arranged the loan, so there's nothing I can tell the police."

"But they think there is…"

"Davis says these people don't take any chances. They'll just get rid of me."

"And Davis is one of them?"

"He *works* for them, but I think he wants out and he's taking me with him. That's all I know, I swear. I don't know where we're going or anything else." They stared at each other for a few long minutes, one hoping she believed what he said, the other wishing she could.

***

George was already in bed when Karl pulled into the driveway. Thelma was still sitting in the living room in her armchair, but she didn't notice the lights of the car. She was thinking about Davis. And how George seemed to blindly trust him, a man who was apparently involved with people worse than loan sharks. Why would someone like that want to help her husband? He must be doing this to save his own skin. And if George really was in danger, why would Davis drop him off at the house for the night? Was Davis going to leave the country without him?

Karl walked in the door and she glanced up at him. "Where's Dad?" he asked. "Did you throw him out?"

"No, dear." She sighed. "He's gone to bed."

"What did he tell you?"

Thelma bit her lip. She couldn't share her thoughts with her son. She told him that his dad said Davis was a good guy and would take care of him. "I think the plan is to convince them that your dad has disappeared. The more you think about it, the more it sounds like Davis is in a lot of trouble too."

"What do you know about the people he works for?"

Thelma shook her head. "You know your dad. He claims they're just money lenders. I think there's something more to it, but..." She took a small breath. "What's he told you?"

"Not much. But I know that Davis really ran the business, he made all the decisions. Ever since he showed up, it was like it was his company." Karl frowned. "What should we do, Mom?"

"We go along with the plan, that's all we can do."

***

When George came downstairs the following morning, he looked relaxed, probably a combination of a good night's sleep in his own bed and having the family around.

"What time is Davis coming?" Thelma asked.

"He said he'd be here by two. I need to pack a bag and grab my passport."

"I've already packed your bag, it's in the corner, and here's your passport."

George hugged her. Over breakfast he opened up a bit more about the plan and told her they were staying at a hog farm in the

Fraser Valley, not far from a small airport in Haney. They'd fly out on a small plane in a few days.

Karl got up around eleven, but his time with his dad was cut short. Davis arrived early. Thelma stood up and hugged George, afraid to let go for fear she may never see him again. George finally broke free. She held his hand as she followed him to the door. "Call me as soon as you get there," she said into his shoulder.

"I will."

Davis raised his eyebrows from the doorway. "Come on, George. Time to go."

George hugged Karl and then headed out the front door and got into the Land Rover. He waved to Thelma and Karl as they pulled into the street. When he looked back at his house, he wondered if he'd ever see it again.

Chapter 13

It was another cold morning. Pat Lossan sipped a coffee and waited in a boardroom at the Regional Gang Prosecutors' office on Carrall Street in Vancouver. A moment later, Paul Bolton appeared, looking uncharacteristically dishevelled. Lossan greeted his friend with a look of concern, but before he could ask whether there'd been any more threatening calls or anything else, they were joined by Corporal Dennis Kovacs of the RCMP Security Service. Lossan thought he looked even more tired than Bolton. The older man settled himself on the far side of the table and glanced over a few papers while they waited for Douglas McDonald, the regional prosecutor. A few minutes later, an overweight man with white hair and a beard to match walked in and introduced himself. McDonald nodded to Kovacs and then settled into the nearest chair.

For the next several minutes, Lossan briefly highlighted the key points of the Koehle case. McDonald listened as he took notes and didn't interrupt. Kovacs didn't look up from his papers.

When it was quiet again, McDonald looked up at Lossan. "We've been involved in the prosecution of several cases involving Vancouver gangs, and Corporal Kovacs and his associates are currently involved in numerous ongoing investigations. Mr. Bolton, what's your role here?"

Before Bolton could answer, Lossan leaned forward. "Mr. Bolton is a forensic accountant working with us on this case. His firm is also the trustee in bankruptcy of Goldstate, and he's the reason we're involved. He's received a series of threatening phone calls and"—Lossan glanced at Bolton—"yesterday his girlfriend was almost run over by a red car. We believe it might be related to this investigation."

McDonald took off his reading glasses. "Mr. Bolton, I apologize. We take this matter very seriously. But it's unlikely the gang are involved in the phone calls or the car incident; it's not their style. The calls are more likely from a family member, an employee, or someone affected by the bank calling the company loans."

Bolton was used to the insensitivity and bureaucracy of the police and the Crown. The phone calls were one thing, but the attack on Terry could have been fatal. He wasn't sure if it was another attempt to get at him, but he felt helpless and knew he couldn't protect her all the time. They could be watching his apartment. They might follow her. He'd decided that being part of the investigation team may help him learn more about what was really going on.

Lossan could see his friend was uncomfortable with the talk about his personal life. "So, what's next?" Lossan said.

McDonald looked around the room. "We're interested in the gang. I recommend your investigation be continued under the direction of the RCMP Security Service. There's no case without Koehle's testimony. We'll apply for a warrant for Koehle's arrest and put a tail on Davis." McDonald looked at Lossan. "What more can you tell us about Davis?"

"He manages their business interests and developed the Koehle connection. I expect they told him to clean it up and shut it down. It must have been a surprise when the bank called the loan. Sounds like Davis dropped the ball."

"Was the gang owed money?" asked McDonald.

Lossan shook his head. "It's tough to tell exactly how much at this time; all we know is that large sums of money were funnelled in and out of the company in the last three years."

Kovacs looked up from the file he was reading. "Davis is a hard case, but not an enforcer. Too smart for that. We know that some of Davis's associates own companies that have been funnelling money into Koehle's company for some time. Pubs, nightclubs, payday loan companies, home builders, mortgage brokers and, of all things, a hog farm. All have criminal records."

McDonald looked at the group and said, "Corporal Kovacs can arrange for surveillance of the Koehle family as well as Davis's boss, McVittie." McDonald stood up, signalling the end of the meeting.

***

George Koehle's mind stayed on his family as they drove away from his home, and the car was quiet until Davis switched on the radio.

"Did you explain everything as we discussed?" Davis asked.

"Yes, but she didn't believe me. And she's not happy. You know women, always more questions."

Davis leaned back in his seat and stared at the road ahead. "Don't worry, soon you and I will be on a beach in Costa Rica."

They headed out to the freeway toward Haney. George was thinking about the farm he would be staying at. He'd never been to a hog farm before.

As they pulled off the freeway, George started to pay attention to where he was going. After about eight kilometres they took a left off Lougheed Highway and then turned right onto Hale Road. They were in the middle of the country, farmland everywhere. They stayed on the same road for about five kilometres. George noticed signs for farms but no street signs. They came to a cattle grid and then the road became a gravel path. There were rows of blueberry bushes on either side of them. Eventually, they came to a sign that said Banjeeta Farm. Davis told George to get out and open the gate. Once Davis drove through, George shut the gate behind them and got back in the car. They drove past a small house. "That's the manager's house. It'll be your home for the next few days," Davis said.

George was looking around. He didn't see any hogs. And there was no smell, like he'd imagined there should be. "This doesn't look like a hog farm," he said.

Davis smirked. "Change of plans," he said. "Let's go and meet the boys."

George looked across at Davis in shock. Was he taking him directly to the gang? He gripped the door handle of the Land Rover.

"Relax, we'll be there soon." They drove down the gravel road and came to a series of buildings and a farmhouse, where they parked. Three men came out of the farmhouse to meet them. They were all well over six feet tall, powerfully built, and each had a long grey beard and wore a white turban. "Come on, George. Let's say hi." Reluctantly George got out and stood by the side of the vehicle, while Davis walked across to greet the men.

"Mr. Alan, you made it. How are you?"

"I'm fine, Harman." Davis turned to the second man. "Charan, how are you?"

"Greetings, Mr. Alan. I don't think you've met our father, Gurdev Sangha."

Davis went to shake Gurdev's hand, but the father held back.

"Sorry," Charan said. "My father doesn't speak English. And I tried to explain the situation. He's not happy but said if it was only for a few days, and your man doesn't wander around, then he could live with it."

Davis turned to George and introduced his friends. Davis thanked the brothers again, especially given the last-minute change of plans. George wondered how well Davis knew them. And had Davis ever really intended on taking him to a hog farm? Or was the whole thing a lie in case George told his family too much, which, of course, he had. He felt a rare surge of anger. This was *his* life. What right did Davis have to lie to him about it? He was about to confront the man when Charan began speaking.

"We left the key on the kitchen counter, and there's food in the fridge." He turned to George. "Please do not wander too far; we are closed for the season and have security at night." Charan grinned. "Our guard dog is not friendly." Davis and Charan shared a laugh, and then Charan turned back to George. "Seriously, please do not wander from the manager's house at night." George assured him he wouldn't. Charan smiled. "And if you need anything, come to our house and knock."

Davis thanked them again and promised George wouldn't be any trouble.

George and Davis got into the Land Rover and headed back to the manager's house, which was really a converted shed, about five by six metres. But it was clean and tidy and had some natural sunlight from the window at the far end. There was a single bed with clean sheets and blankets, a tiny stove and half-sized fridge, and a little table and two chairs on one side. There was a separate room with a toilet and a small, full-length shower. George opened the fridge and found a large container of blueberries. In the kitchen cupboard there was some old cereal, a few tea bags, half a jar of instant coffee and some condiments.

George sat on the bed, which was quite firm, and opened a drawer in the table next to it. There he found a crib board, a deck of cards and three dog-eared paperbacks. He pulled out the books. *Bonecrack* by Dick Francis, *Mr. Majestyk* by Elmore Leonard, and *Tinker Tailor Soldier Spy* by John le Carré. He looked up as Davis came in carrying two bags of groceries. He set the bags on the table and looked at his watch. "I've gotta go. If something comes up, talk to Charan, but only if it's an emergency. The less they know, the better."

"Davis, wait. I want to trust you. I mean, I do, it's just—"

"Look, in a few days, we'll both be on a plane. Till then, stay put, don't go anywhere, don't try and contact anyone, just *relax*, and don't do anything stupid. Remember I've got as much at stake as you have. I've got to go; I've still got a lot of planning to do."

"Okay, okay." As he was leaving George couldn't help but wonder what planning he had in mind. He was about to ask him and decided he wouldn't get a straight answer. Where was he going?

After Davis left, George stretched out on the bed. He'd put complete faith in Davis. For all he knew the gang could be on their way. He shook those thoughts away and tried to relax, but his mind kept wandering. Davis wasn't telling him everything. And what could he do, he didn't even know where he was. Somewhere between Haney and Maple Ridge. He remembered the sign Banjeeta Farm. What was the name of the road they turned down after they left the Lougheed? George sat up and looked around for some paper. He found none, but there was a pencil in the drawer. He picked up one of the books, flipped it open and started to write things down on the inside back cover. *Yes, that's it, Hale Road.*

When he'd written all he could remember, George decided to go for a walk. It was still light out, and he figured talking a walk would clear his head and give him a better idea of where he was located. He took the key and locked the door. It was 3:00 p.m. He followed the road that looped past the farmhouse and toward the fields until he came to a wooden gate on one side. There were a few cows at the far end, all lying down. They had a simple life, and at this moment, he envied them.

George leaned over the fence and thought back to when he was a child. Things were easy then, no worries. When he first got married, life was good. His problems started when he got into real estate.

He carried on walking down the road. In the distance he noticed a structure at the side of the road. As he got closer, he saw it was a telephone booth. A strange place for a phone booth, in the middle of nowhere. He opened the door and picked up the phone, expecting the line to be dead, vandalized by some kids, but it worked. He looked at the number on the phone dial and memorized it. He'd write it down inside the book when he got back.

He looked at his watch again and realized he'd been gone over half an hour. Time to head back. Maybe he'd come back here in the morning and phone Thelma, let her know where he was. He walked back to the house. He'd make himself something to eat and read one of the books. There was no television, not even a radio. George locked the door behind him. Then he opened the fridge and tried to figure out what he'd make for supper.

Chapter 14

Dennis Kovacs was concerned. The old RCMP Security Service corporal had been waiting for news, but there'd been no sign of Davis. And the warrant for George Koehle's arrest hadn't come through yet. The judge wanted more evidence of gang involvement and wasn't convinced that Koehle was in any real danger.

As Kovacs read the brief note from the judge, he knew the chances of finding Koehle weren't good. He also wondered if Davis was still alive. He knew McVittie wouldn't have a problem getting rid of both of them if he felt threatened.

Kovacs set the note on his desk, closed his eyes and rubbed the bridge of his nose. He'd have to call that enthusiastic young Mountie, Lossan. He picked up the phone and waited for the receptionist to patch him through.

"Lossan here."

"Yeah. This is Kovacs, over at the RCMP Security Service. Listen, the judge wants more evidence for a warrant. I think by the end of the week if Davis and Koehle haven't shown up, we should pay a visit to Koehle's wife."

After they hung up, Kovacs studied the judge's note for a few more minutes and then leaned back in his chair. He tended to assume the worst and figured both bodies would show up sooner rather than later. Gangs liked to send a message to people that crossed them and maintained their power by intimidation, threats and ruthlessness. He remembered a case, from years ago, of a high-profile gang member who'd let it be known that he wanted to leave the gang. The guy was newly married with a kid. A week later, his charred remains were found inside his burnt-out pickup, parked across the street from the new home he was having built.

∗

At 4:00 p.m., Kovacs sat at his desk, staring at some papers he'd been shuffling around all day, but not taking anything in. Something about this Koehle case was sticking with him, and he was finding it hard to focus on anything else. When he heard the phone, he snatched it before the second ring. Finally. It was the judge's clerk advising that he'd signed the warrant. He'd have to call Lossan again. McDonald had been firm about that. The RCMP were to stay involved. Kovacs had worked with RCMP before on gang investigations and was troubled by their by-the-book approach and concern for individuals' rights. Lossan didn't strike him as any different. In fact, he may be worse, too much of a boyscout. Having spent thirty years chasing criminals, he didn't see any point in being nice. Two divorces and losing a partner in a gang shootout had made him cynical beyond repair. He'd seen too many gang members go free because they hired a smart lawyer, or some judge didn't believe they were fully apprised of their rights when being interviewed. He dialled Lossan's number again.

"We got the warrant for Koehle," he told the young officer, "but no surveillance. You know how it is. Budget cuts."

∗

Early the next morning, Kovacs and Lossan pulled up in front of the Koehle's residence. Kovacs turned off the engine. "I'll ask the questions, okay?"

Lossan gave him a wide smile. "Sure, boss." He popped a stick of gum into his mouth and opened his door.

Kovacs closed his eyes for a second as though he was praying for patience, then stepped out of the car. They approached the house together and Kovacs banged on the front door, which was opened by a small woman in her fifties.

"Mrs. Koehle?"

"Yes?"

"I'm Corporal Dennis Kovacs of the RCMP Security Service, and this is Corporal Pat Lossan of the RCMP Commercial Crime Division. We have a warrant for your husband's arrest." Kovacs handed her the warrant.

Thelma took a small step back. "George isn't here."

They walked past her into the living room. When she recovered, Thelma almost ran to catch up with them. "Let me get my son." She continued into the hallway and called out his name. As she scanned the warrant, her son came down the stairs. "This is Karl. These gentlemen are from the police and they have a warrant for your dad's arrest." Thelma swallowed hard as she handed him the warrant. Karl looked stunned. He took the paper and read it like a man who needed something to do to keep from crying.

The younger cop looked like a giant in the small living room. Thelma didn't know whether to ask him to sit down, so she just stood there, staring. The other cop, the older one, was looking around the room. Finally, he turned to her. "When did you last see your husband?"

Thelma looked at her son but said nothing.

Kovacs let out an impatient breath. "This may come as a surprise, Mrs. Koehle, but your husband's company, Goldstate, has been used as a front for various illegal activities by a Vancouver gang. We've been brought in by the RCMP to assist in the investigation."

Kovacs noticed her eyes blink at the word *gang*. Karl, who'd been standing at the bottom of the stairs, with his hands on hips, moved back ever so slightly and almost tripped. He caught himself on the bannister.

Kovacs scratched the patch of silver hair near his temple. "Look lady, this isn't time to play games. Your husband's life is at stake. This gang, well, they don't mess around. They'll make sure of your husband's silence."

Thelma looked like she was going to say something, but Karl moved to her side and said, "You're saying my dad is mixed up with a gang? I don't believe it. You're trying to scare us."

Kovacs turned his dark glare toward the young man. "Do you know Alan Davis? If you do, you know he's a gang member. It's his gang that's been using Goldstate to launder drug money."

"Alan Davis?" Thelma asked, one hand pressed lightly to her chest.

Kovacs nodded. "It's unlikely your husband was involved in the money laundering, but it's difficult to believe he wasn't aware of it."

Karl moved closer to Kovacs, his face red. "I don't believe you. You're making this all up. Dad wouldn't let this happen."

Lossan spoke up. "Mrs. Koehle, your husband is listed as a director of two companies owned by the gang."

Thelma closed her eyes.

"Look," Kovacs said, "His life's at risk. When they find him, they'll kill him. We can only protect him if we find him before they do."

Karl moved another step closer to Kovacs. "I think you've both said enough. Now leave us alone."

"I'm afraid we can't do that, son," Kovacs said.

Lossan looked at Thelma apologetically. "We need to search the house."

She nodded, then turned to her son. "Come on, Karl." She touched his arm, and he allowed her to guide him to the kitchen.

Meanwhile, Lossan went upstairs, and Kovacs headed to the basement and then out into the backyard where he checked the garage and the garden shed. They were both back in less than fifteen minutes.

Karl was sitting at the kitchen table with a cup of coffee. He glared at them when they came in the room. "Satisfied?"

"Mrs. Koehle, has your husband been here in the last three weeks?" Kovacs asked.

Karl stood up. "We don't have to answer any of your questions. Just leave."

Kovacs ignored Karl. There was nothing more he'd have liked than to arrest the little jerk for obstruction of justice. But he'd seen the way Karl had looked at his mother when he told her about the gang and what they'd do to her husband. Karl knew more than he was telling, and Kovacs figured that sooner or later he'd lead them to Davis.

He turned and faced Thelma again. "I didn't see your husband's passport, Mrs. Koehle." Thelma blotted her face with a tissue but said nothing. Kovacs grimaced. "Well, ma'am, in the event you change your mind and want to help your husband, this is how you can reach us." He set his business card on the table next to Lossan's, and they both headed back to the front hall.

On the drive back, Kovacs commented on Thelma's reaction when the word *gang* was mentioned. Lossan nodded. "And clearly, Karl knows Davis," he said.

"I think chances are good we're gonna hear from Koehle," Kovacs said. "That is, if he's still alive."

***

Thelma hadn't moved from her spot in the kitchen. She didn't want to believe what she'd heard. She knew George had gotten in over his head, but she'd never thought her husband was a criminal. Now she didn't know what to believe. Or whether she'd ever see him again.

"Mom." Thelma looked up, startled. Karl was staring at her from across the table. "Mom, don't worry. Davis is okay. And I think he's really trying to help."

Thelma just stared at him. Her son was like her husband, too trusting. If it came to Davis looking after himself or her husband, she knew what would happen. She looked down at her tea and ignored whatever he was saying. She didn't want to waste time arguing; he wouldn't listen to her anyway. Instead, she drifted back to the conversation with the police. Why would they go to all this trouble to get a warrant and make up a story about a gang? They knew about Davis's background. They'd been through the books. She frowned. *They aren't interested in George. They've stumbled onto something much bigger.* She looked at the cards the police had left on the table. That's why someone from the Criminal Intelligence Service was involved.

"Mom? Are you listening to me?"

Thelma looked up at her son. "Yes, dear."

Karl got up and moved to the counter, picked up the coffee pot and poured the rest into his mug. As she watched him, Thelma felt the sudden desire to hold him on her lap as she used to. To protect him from the world. He'd always idolized his father. And she'd never said a bad word about George in front of him. She frowned. Perhaps protecting him so much had been a mistake. He was twenty-three and still living at home. Most of his friends had steady jobs, some were even married.

Karl returned to the table and sat down. "I need to talk to Davis, tell him what happened. We just can't sit here and do nothing, can we?"

No, she thought, *we can't, but for once I'm going to handle this.* She wanted to tell Karl to keep quiet. But she knew he wouldn't listen to her. Karl was impulsive, and like his father, he lied to her.

She'd have to wait until he left the house. "I need time to think, son."

"Well, I'm going to see Davis." Karl got up and headed out the front door. A few seconds later, she heard his car pull out of the driveway.

Thelma picked up the phone in the hallway and dialled the number from one of the business cards. The phone rang and rang. Finally, there was a recorded message telling her that Corporal Kovacs was unavailable. She pressed zero and waited for the operator to pick up. Then she left a message asking him to call her as soon as possible.

Kovacs was just pulling out of the parking lot at the RCMP Security Service when dispatch relayed the message on the radio for him to call Mrs. Koehle back. Rather than call, he gunned it and headed toward the Koehle residence. He parked his car a block away, on a side street, walked to the house and knocked on the door. Thelma Koehle opened it and glanced outside. Then she leaned close to Kovacs and said in a low voice, "My husband was here yesterday. He left with Davis around one thirty. He was going to stay at a farm somewhere, out in the valley, and then fly somewhere."

Kovacs nodded. "I take it your son's gone?"

"Yes."

"Can you tell me anything else?"

"Just that I remember George saying it was a hog farm near Haney."

Thelma watched as Kovacs walked back to his vehicle, got into the driver's seat and picked up a phone. She went back in the house and sat down in her favourite chair. For years she'd turned a blind eye to her husband's business activities. She'd stood by him in the past when his business had failed. This time he'd got people from the church involved, and many invested their life savings in the business. This time he'd gone too far. Doing business with a gang. Risking his life. And now in hiding and running from a gang. Worst of all, he was putting his trust in the very man who'd introduced him to the gang. George would probably end up going to prison. *But only if the gang doesn't catch up with him*, she thought. She shook her head to clear it of such thoughts. But this didn't work. Her mind went immediately to Karl. He had a habit of sticking his nose into things, trying to help his dad, when all too often he only made matters worse. His blind trust in Davis worried her even more.

Thelma closed her eyes, placed her hands together and bowed her head. As she'd done so many times before, she prayed that George would be all right and that no harm would come to either him or her son. Instead of finding peace in the prayer, it only made her think of her church and what all this would mean for her and George. Quickly, she dismissed the thought from her head. While the church was an important part of her life, her family was more important. She wished she should confide in someone, but she was too embarrassed and ashamed to share her fears with even her closest friends. Even the church elders that she respected were duty bound to share her concerns with each other.

This was something she couldn't share with anyone else. She had to stay strong for her husband and her son and hope that the police would find George. She looked at her wedding picture, hung above the mantle. Maybe she should have listened to her parents all those years ago. But it was too late for regrets.

Chapter 15

Davis hung up the phone and leaned back into his leather couch. As good as it felt to be home, he knew he shouldn't have risked coming back. Especially after the call he'd just gotten from Karl, telling him the police had visited the family home with a warrant for George's arrest. Davis had expected a police visit before too long but thought he had more time. George might have shared the details of his plan with his wife and if she talked to the police, they'd assume he was hiding at the Troyer farm and start a search. Once Troyer's farm was raided, McVittie would know that he'd been playing games and come looking for him for sure. He needed to change his plans. They might be coming for him already.

George, on the other hand, was safe for the time being, so long as he stayed put and didn't do anything stupid. No one in the gang knew about Davis's connection to the Sangha family. Davis knew he'd have to arrange for someone else to take George to the airport. He couldn't risk going back to the farm. Maybe he should change the airport. Davis stood up and stared out the window. Why was he going to all this trouble when he'd be better off telling the gang where George was?

He walked over to an end table, picked up the phone and dialled the number for Pitt Meadows airport. It was a small airfield, catering mostly to private aircraft, about fifty kilometres out of the city, bordering the Fraser River. His friend Parsons had a plane hangered there.

"Hey, Parsons," Davis said when his friend answered. "May need to change my plans. Any chance I can fly out of a different airport? Somewhere small but still in the valley?" Parsons told him he'd call him back later when he'd had time to make the changes.

Davis hung up and looked out the front window again. The police could be watching his place too. He needed a safe place to think and plan. He headed into his bedroom and picked up his already packed bag. He just needed a few more things. His phone rang.

It was Karl again. "Is it true what the police said? You're part of a gang?"

"For God's sake. Not now, kid. We can meet later."

"I'm right outside. And I'm not leaving until we talk."

Stupid idiot. How the hell did the kid find out where he lived? Did he stake out every Davis in the phone directory? Kid was smarter than he thought. Goddammit. Davis shifted the receiver to his other ear. "How do you know you weren't followed?" Before Karl could answer, Davis said, "Meet me at Mario's in thirty minutes."

"I'm not going anywhere, Davis."

The kid was going to attract attention. "Fine. I'll be out in five." Davis looked out the window. A red Mustang was now parked on the other side of the street. He didn't have time for this, but the sooner he dealt with Karl, the sooner he could start worrying about himself. He grabbed his coat and bag and headed out the front door. He didn't see anyone suspicious as he crossed the street and got into the car. "Drive," he said. "Head for the parking lot on the east side of the Brentwood mall." Davis turned his side mirror out and watched the traffic behind.

"Why the mall?"

Davis wanted to hit the kid, but he took a breath and calmed himself. "Because the best place to lose a tail is the left turn lane into the mall, off Willingdon."

Karl didn't say anything else, but he checked his mirrors several times and pulled into the left turn lane as ordered. There were three cars ahead of them and five or six behind. Karl slowed as they approached the green left turn light and almost stopped, so the car behind him slammed on his brakes and hit the horn. Then, as the green light turned to amber, Karl waited until oncoming traffic was starting and then accelerated, making the turn at the last minute. There was no way any car behind him could turn left without hitting the oncoming traffic. Davis looked back to see if he recognized any of the vehicles. He wasn't sure.

They headed for the other side of the mall and drove up to the top floor of the indoor garage and parked. They waited in silence for a few minutes. No vehicle came into the parking lot on that level.

"All right, kid. What do you want?" Davis asked.

"I want to know why you're helping my dad. Why not just get rid of him, like the cops said you gang members would?"

"I've asked myself the same question."

Karl's jaw dropped.

"Take it easy. I'm not planning on killing him or handing him over to the gang, although that's what I should do."

Karl's bravado seemed to be running thin, now that he was alone in the car with Davis, talking about murder. "Why are you doing this?" he asked.

"I have my reasons. They got nothing to do with you or your dad. Now the cops are looking for your dad; it won't be long before the gang hears about it and they'll be doing the same thing. They'll be looking for me as well. Probably already are."

Davis was certain they'd been followed and that the police had been watching both homes. "You can't go home now, it may not be safe. Call your mom and tell her to leave too. Get out of town, stay out of sight and don't contact anyone. Your mom will need protection. You too, for that matter."

Karl looked very pale in the fluorescent light shining through the windshield. "What do you mean?"

"Look, kid, do I have to spell it out for you? The gang could soon be looking for you or your mom. Anyone that knows where your dad is. Understand?"

"Yeah. What are you going to do?"

"You're going to drop me off at the Villa Hotel."

Karl swallowed, but some of the colour seemed to return to his face now that Davis appeared to have a plan and was concerned about him and his mother. He turned on the engine and headed south on Willingdon to the Villa Hotel. The short drive passed in silence.

Davis got out of the car and headed into the hotel. Karl stared at him for a few minutes and then pulled away. Davis watched the Mustang as it drove to the end of the street and turned left back toward Willingdon. He ordered a coffee at the coffee bar, sat down and drank it. Ten minutes later, he went outside and hailed a cab.

"Where to, sir?"

"The 401 Inn on Boundary."

"That's not as good a hotel as this one, sir."

"I know, but that's where I'm going."

He checked into the 401 Inn on Boundary under the name Sparling and paid cash. Once in his room, Davis sat down on his bed and called Parsons again. No answer. He hung up. By this time, the police would be searching the farm and the gang would know what was going on. Davis closed his eyes. The game was almost over.

Chapter 16

Kovacs asked to be put through to Lossan, who was on the line in less than a minute. Kovacs explained the visit with Thelma Koehle. "There's the Troyer farm out that way," he told Lossan. "It's a hog farm and he's a gang member. We searched the place a few years ago. Smell of the pigs made tracking a human almost impossible."

They agreed that Lossan would arrange to keep an eye on the farm until they were able to obtain a warrant and organize a full search with tracker dogs.

Less than twenty-four hours later, Lossan and Kovacs stood in the briefing room in front of six Mounties. Kovacs pointed to a wall chart with a map of the Troyer farmhouse and buildings and an outline of his plan.

Lossan had sent an officer to Thelma Koehle's residence to get a piece of her husband's clothing for the dogs to sniff. Troyer would be taken into custody. They didn't want him talking to anyone while they were conducting the search.

Someone asked if the black-and-white photo of Koehle was recent. That's when Kovacs realized no one had met him before. There was a lot they hadn't thought through and a lot that could go wrong. But they didn't have the luxury of time. The sooner they got out there, the better.

Kovacs warned the officers that it wouldn't be easy. The smell could be overwhelming at times. There was a cesspool used to store the pig excrement, and the treated waste was sprayed onto the fields using a mobile sprinkler. There were also dead boxes—wooden containers that were filled with rotting hogs. "You'll all have masks. And weather's on our side. It won't be as bad as it was that summer when we searched it before."

Another hand went up. "Sir, will we be required to drag the cesspool or examine the boxes?"

"Not at this time, son." Kovacs looked at Lossan who'd read his thoughts. *If George is in either of those places, we're too late.*

Kovacs looked over the group. There were no more questions. "All right. We'll rendezvous about one mile from the farm site, at the lay-by heading east on Dewdney Trunk Road at 4:00 p.m."

***

Kovacs and Lossan arrived at the rendezvous point in Maple Ridge at 3:50 p.m. The other vans were already there. The gate to the farm was closed and padlocked. Lossan waved to someone in one of the other vans and the officer got out of his vehicle with a large set of bolt cutters, broke the padlock and opened the gate. Kovacs led the convoy of vans to the main farm. They parked near the house and Kovacs got out of his van, walked up the steps to the front porch and banged loudly on the door. There was no answer. He instructed one of the men to batter the door down, when a voice shouted, "Hey! What are you guys doing?"

Kovacs looked around. A tall young man, unshaven and dirty looking with long tangled hair, started walking toward him. Undeterred by the three police vans or the men handling the dogs, the young man stopped when he reached Kovacs. "What the hell do you think you're doing? This is private property."

Kovacs flashed his badge. "We have a warrant to search the property." He handed him a copy of the warrant.

The man wiped his dirty hands on the back of his jeans and took the paper but didn't read it. "The owner's not here. Come back in the morning."

Kovacs smiled. "It doesn't work that way, son. What's your name and what do you do here?"

The young man seemed to be deciding something, but after a moment, he said, "Fred Troyer. My dad owns the farm."

"Is your dad around?"

"Everyone's gone for the day. Like I said, you should come back when my dad's here."

"Where is he?"

"He's downtown and won't be back till the morning."

"Well, in that case, we'll have to start without him."

"What are you looking for anyway?"

"A man named George Koehle. We have a warrant for his arrest."

"He isn't here. No one's here but me and the hogs."

Kovacs ignored him and gestured toward the door. "You can save us all some time and start by unlocking the front door. Then you can take us on a tour of the property."

"Why should I?"

Kovacs had had enough and nodded to the officer to break down the door. Just as he was about to swing the ram, Troyer shouted, "All right! All right! I'll open it."

Kovacs signalled to the other officers who proceeded to start their search. Two officers entered the farmhouse. The two dog handlers each gave their dog a sniff of Koehle's shirt and then let them off their leashes. They started to sniff the ground and then slowly started walking away from the group. One of the dogs headed in the direction of the cesspool located at the back of one of the larger pens.

Kovacs and Lossan pulled their face masks out of their bags and put them on. They headed for the first building. Kovacs had forgotten how squalid the pig pens were. There must have been over two hundred hogs squeezed into the barn. And Kovacs knew from his last visit that the pigs spent over eighteen hours a day in the pens during the fall and winter months. He grimaced and thanked whatever god was out there that he hadn't been born a pig.

Chapter 17

George was making himself dinner at the manager's house. *Tinker Tailor Soldier Spy* was open on the counter, and while he waited for things to cook, he leaned over it and read. George couldn't remember the last time he'd read a book like this. He liked spy movies but never seemed to have the patience to read a novel.

After dinner, he was restless. A few chapters before bed might take his mind off his problem, it might even help him sleep. As he read, he began to recognize some of the characters from the movie. He thought about the scene where Smiley kept taking off his thick dark glasses and polishing them. Slightly stooped, with thinning hair, he always faded into the background and disliked attention. He didn't look like a spy, more like an accountant or librarian who'd been put out to pasture. *Appearances can be deceptive*, George thought. Davis didn't look like a gangster either. At least when his sleeves weren't rolled up.

George was drawn into the story, as if he were there in London, walking along the same streets and looking at the same places as the characters in the book. For the first time in weeks, he forgot about his problems. A banging on his door made him jump and almost drop his book. "Hello? Who is it?"

"Hello, Mr. George, it's Charan from the farm. Mr. Alan phoned and asked me to remind you that he will be picking you up at two o'clock tomorrow afternoon."

"Okay, thank you."

"Good night, Mr. George."

Davis was likely to show up earlier than planned. If George was going to do anything, he needed to do it in the morning. He sat on the bed and reached for his jacket. He checked the contents of his wallet. He had about eighty dollars in bills, two credit cards, a driver's licence, an old photo of Thelma and Karl, and a few business cards. One was Paul Bolton's, the guy from Kinsey he'd met with Davis. It had an office phone number and an address on Burrard Street in downtown Vancouver. George stared at the name. *You're the reason I'm in this mess*, he thought. But he knew that wasn't true. It wasn't Bolton's fault. It was his. He thought back to the time he'd first met Bolton. He knew he was just doing his job, and if it hadn't been him, it would have been someone else acting for the bank. Sooner or later, the bank would have done something. It was easier for him to blame Bolton for his problems than to admit the truth. He remembered the times Thelma told him to face up to his problems and not blame someone else. She was right.

He'd gotten in with the wrong people when the business was struggling, and now he couldn't get out. He knew his business had been used by the gang. He knew Davis was running drug money through the business. When the bank called the loan, he tried to look after his investors. All Bolton was doing was his job. He remembered the meeting several weeks ago in his office on Hastings Street. Bolton in his slick suit with his fancy hair and manicured nails. These weren't things George usually noticed, but perhaps he was looking for things to hate about the man. He looked down at his own ragged nails and sighed. He really should take better care of himself. And Bolton hadn't been all bad. The accountant had told him he should call if he had any questions. On impulse, George wrote the number down in the back of his book and put the card back in his wallet.

Then he stared at the darkness outside. He probably wouldn't sleep at all tonight knowing Davis would be arriving tomorrow to either fly him down to Costa Rica or kill him. George had decided, somewhere between dinner and now, that he couldn't trust Davis. And that's when he'd started to form a plan, though not much of one. He wasn't sure where he was going but, come first thing tomorrow, he'd be gone. He picked up the book again and started reading.

A few pages later, realizing he wasn't taking anything in, he put the book down again. Something else had occurred to him. He couldn't remember the last time he'd given much thought to Thelma or Karl. They could be in danger too. He'd been too busy worrying about himself. He picked up the book again and forced himself to read. He was determined not to think about it.

Chapter 18

Kovacs left two men searching the barn and wandered out to the open field, where Troyer caught up with him. In the distance he could see the cesspool. It was an open-air pit about twenty by ten metres. "How deep is it?" Kovacs asked Troyer.

"Three feet."

Kovacs watched him walk back to the house. *Probably to phone his old man*, he thought. The old man would go crazy. The thought of cops crawling all over his farm would make him mad. He'd been there the last time they'd raided the farm, refused to let them on the property and started to fight. He was arrested and stuck in the back of a van while they carried out the search. Four hours later, they took him downtown and charged him. He ended up spending the night in prison. Just as well he wasn't at the farm this time. Kovacs had hoped that the old man would be there and he could arrest him for failing to cooperate. He was tempted to arrest the son. When he told Lossan that's what he planned to do, he finally listened to reason. The kid had cooperated and there wasn't much he could do, and he knew that pretty soon the gang would hear about their search. If they weren't looking for Davis before, they would be now.

But it seemed there wasn't any sign of George Koehle. Although all the buildings were lit, and they were able to check them thoroughly, there was a lot of land to cover, and the flashlights weren't much use. There seemed to be lots of unsheltered areas where garbage and animal remains had been stored. One of the dogs had found a few old bones that they'd have forensics look at, but chances were, they were from a hog.

Kovacs looked at Lossan. "I'm beginning to think this may be a wild goose chase."

"You don't think Davis deliberately mentioned the farm knowing George would tell his wife."

Kovacs shrugged. "I wouldn't put anything past Davis."

"Or he could be dead already and they dumped the body somewhere else."

"I don't know, but we're running out of ideas. Unless he's in there." Kovacs pointed to the cesspool.

"The dogs keep coming back here, but maybe that's just the smell? Let's drain it in the morning. In the meantime, let's shut down the place and not let anyone in or out."

Kovacs grimaced. "It's gonna be a hell of a job draining it."

Kovacs arranged for officers to stay behind while Lossan headed back to his van and made a call on the radio phone. A few minutes later, he walked over to Kovacs. "Seems Thelma Koehle contacted Burnaby RCMP. Said her son warned her to leave home and go straight to the police."

Kovacs thought about this. "You think the gang threatened him?"

Lossan shrugged. "The boys said they really didn't get much out of her other than Karl seemed scared and warned her not to go back home. I'll meet with her first thing in the morning." He smiled suddenly. "I guess I won't be here to drain the cesspool."

Kovacs frowned. "How come I always get the shit jobs? I guess I was born lucky."

They met Fred Troyer in front of the farmhouse and told him they were leaving but were going to leave officers on site until they'd drained the cesspool in the morning. In the meantime, any access to the farm would be subject to police approval. They were also going to deny any access to the cesspool for the time being.

Kovacs stared at Troyer and wondered what he really knew about his dad. "We'll see you here bright and early in the morning, son."

"Wait a minute. My dad wants me to see some identification from you guys."

"We showed you already."

Troyer looked uncomfortable. "I didn't remember where you were from—"

They both showed their IDs again. This time Troyer leaned forward and read the badges. "What's CISC?"

Kovacs smiled. "Ask your dad."

***

Tom Troyer had never seen his boss as angry as he was when their meeting had been interrupted by a call from Troyer's son, Fred, telling him that the police had just raided their farm looking for George Koehle. The veins on the side of McVittie's neck bulged and his face had turned purple. "Goddam Davis! He was supposed to deal with him by now. I'll kill him when I get my hands on him."

McVittie had called one of his enforcers. "Find that son of a bitch Koehle. And that traitor Davis too."

"How long do we stake out Davis's place, boss?"

"Until you find him, idiot. And don't screw this up or you'll have me to deal with. Understand?"

"Right away, boss."

McVittie poured himself another coffee and sat down at his desk. *What's that bastard up to*, he thought. Davis had never killed anyone before, but he'd done some bad stuff. McVittie dumped a spoon of sugar in his coffee and frowned. Davis wasn't a snitch—why would he care about George Koehle? He stirred his coffee slowly as his thoughts turned darker. Davis knew the business better than anyone.

Was that it? Was he helping someone muscle in on the gang's territory? McVittie sipped his coffee and nodded to himself. Davis had been acting strange lately. He'd always been a loner. He was smart, ran the gang like a business and had made them a lot of money, but something wasn't right. McVittie had never really liked him. *And now, I don't trust him. He's not one of us.*

McVittie had never set out to build anything. More of an opportunist, he'd bullied his way into the gang and then slowly took charge, more often by intimidation and threats than anything. Davis was different from the rest of the gang, and McVittie never really understood him.

McVittie had never given any thought to the future, nor had he any desire to spend the money he had. He just liked being in charge and telling people what to do. He couldn't imagine any other life. Anyway, it was a little too late for that. He wondered who would take over after he'd gone. Davis had the smarts to take over, and at one point he was convinced that was his goal. He knew there was no one else in the gang that could take over except Davis, but lately he didn't seem interested.

But he knew he'd be a member of the gang for the rest of his life, and he didn't care what happened after that. Like many old gang members, he knew it was too late to change.

***

Thelma Koehle sat in the police interview room and thought about what she'd done. And she felt relieved. Not only because she felt safe and her fears of being followed by a gang member had proved unfounded, but she'd finally taken action. After years of letting her husband go from one business failure to another, she'd realized her blind faith in him had been misplaced and that, maybe, if she'd played some role in his business, she may have been able to prevent him from making so many bad decisions. She thought back to her own mother who'd been dominated by an overbearing husband. *Not me. Not anymore.*

***

Davis sat on the edge of the bed in his motel and called Parsons again. Still no answer. He toyed with the idea of checking on George, but there was no point until he'd finalized flight plans.

It was after 7:00 p.m. when he finally spoke to Parsons and confirmed that he'd meet him at the Langley airport. Davis said he'd be there a little before 2:00 p.m. and wanted to know how much red tape was involved in getting on the plane.

"Where should I meet you?"

"There's a reception area in the small hangar not far from the main building. Don't be late."

"Don't worry, we'll be there." Davis hung up.

He tried calling Charan and finally got through at about eight o'clock. "I need another favour. I won't be able to pick George up tomorrow after all and was hoping you could take him to the Langley airport for me and meet me there at 1:30 p.m."

"Sorry, Mr. Davis. I'm out tomorrow afternoon."

"I wouldn't ask if it wasn't important. Some people are looking for me, so, the less I'm seen in public, the better."

"I can arrange for a taxi to take Mr. George to the Langley airport."

"I'm worried that he's having second thoughts. I'd rather you take him."

"Mr. Alan, are you in trouble? Am I putting myself or my family in danger?"

"I would never put you or your family at risk. There's absolutely no danger in you taking him to the airport. It's not George that's at risk but me."

Davis could tell Charan wasn't happy and hoped he'd just want to get rid of George.

"Okay, we'll drop him off at the airport, that's it."

"That's fine, thank you. I assure you, you're not at risk."

Davis hung up knowing he'd lied yet again. But it was too risky for him. He couldn't force George to go, and if for any reason George changed his mind and decided not to go, he'd just be wasting time. He was getting on the plane with or without him.

Why was he even giving George a second thought? He'd been nothing but a problem from day one. Slowly he realized that, once upon a time, he actually cared about people and wanted to help, especially the underdog. But there came a time when you could only do so much. He'd already gone above and beyond, and if he'd put anyone at risk, it was himself. He might as well have told McVittie to piss off and deal with George himself. He knew McVittie wouldn't let this go and would try and find a way to come after him no matter what. There may come a time when he'd regret his decision. He'd done everything he could for George and the rest was up to him.

Chapter 19

Karl needed to go home. From what Davis had said, he thought he had time before the gang started watching the house. But, just in case, he circled the block a few times, drove around the back of the house and drove down the lane. He parked at the end of his street and slowly walked to his house. He looked up and down the street again. Satisfied, he walked up to the front door, quietly opened it and headed upstairs to pack a bag.

As he was coming down the stairs, he heard a noise. He panicked, knowing this wasn't a break-in, and rushed to the front door. He was grabbed from behind and pulled to the floor. His attacker let go, and as he turned around and looked up, he saw another bigger man raise a small crowbar in his right hand and swing at him. Karl put his arm up and tried to move to one side. The bar came down hard, and he felt a sharp pain throughout his arm. The smaller guy then started kicking him while he lay on the ground. He tried to protect his face with his other arm.

"Just take what you want and go."

"Funny kid. Where's your dad?" said the guy with the crowbar.

"I don't know. He hasn't been here in days."

The big guy holding the crowbar walked over to the front window, looked out and then closed the curtains. "Sit in that chair. No funny business, or I'll hit the other arm."

Karl slowly got to his feet. He could barely move his arm. Pain shot up it from his fingers to his elbow. He slowly turned around and sat in the chair. He tried to rest his left arm on the wing of the armchair, but the arm couldn't support any weight and the pain kept coming in waves.

"You broke my arm."

"We'll break the other one if you don't start talking. Now where's your dad?"

"I don't know. He left with Alan Davis and didn't say where he was going."

"When?"

"A few days ago."

"And you haven't seen them since?"

"Not my dad. But Davis ... I saw him yesterday at his house. I went to ask him where my dad was. He said he was safe and the fewer people that knew where he was, the better."

"So, he wouldn't tell you? That's what you want us to believe, eh?"

"It's the truth."

Still holding the crowbar, the big thug walked over to Karl and bent down. "I'm going to ask you one more time, where's your dad?"

"I don't know, I honestly don't know." Karl raised his right arm to protect himself, but the thug swung the crowbar down onto Karl's left arm again. Karl let out a shout and cradled the arm to his body. He wanted to cry. He closed his eyes, focusing on controlling the pain and maybe even praying.

When he opened his eyes, the big guy was towering over him, still holding the crowbar. "You're coming with us," he said.

Karl stood up, trying to keep his left arm against his body using his right hand. The big guy pointed to the back door. "Lead the way. I'll be right behind you. One wrong move and you get this in the back of the head. If you see a neighbour, just smile."

Karl was bundled into the back of a van parked in the lane at the back of the house. There were no windows or lights. He tried to sit with his back to the side of the van and protect his arm as best he could, but as they began to move, it was easier to let himself slide down and just lie on the floor. He thought he was going to pee his pants. He'd told them everything he knew. Were they keeping him as some sort of way to threaten his dad? And then what use would they have for him? He knew that Davis wouldn't care. He should have listened to him. It was too late now. What had he been thinking?

They drove for about twenty minutes. All the time, Karl concentrated on not peeing his pants. He didn't want to show them how scared he really was. The stop and start of the vehicle, the sharp turns and the odd bump in the road made the journey that much harder. The van finally came to a stop, the back doors opened, and he was told to get out. He slid on his bum to the back of the van, carefully supporting his left arm with his right, and slid off the edge of the van onto the ground.

"Come on, we don't have all day."

Directed to the back of an old house and told to head down some stairs, Karl was led into a bedroom with bars on the windows. The door was locked behind him. There was a wash basin in the corner, which he used to empty his bladder. Upstairs he could hear voices being raised and what sounded like swearing. After a while, someone came down the stairs and into the bedroom. "The boss will see you now."

He was led upstairs into an office. There were papers on the desk, a bookcase and some charts on the wall. One was a map of the west coast of the US, all the way down to Central America. There were lines drawn between different locations. Someone pushed him toward a chair and told him to sit down. After a few minutes, a heavy-set, unshaven man walked in.

"Karl, do you know who I am?"

"No."

"I'm Walter McVittie, and your dad owes me a lot of money. I need to find him and Alan Davis, and you're going to help me."

"I've already told these guys I haven't seen my dad in two days. He said Davis had a plan to fly them out of the country. He didn't say where he was going, just somewhere in the valley. Some farm."

"Keep going."

"Davis said it was only a matter of time before the police raided the farm. Oh, and he said you guys would hear about it pretty quick and would be after him."

"Where did you last see him?"

"The Villa Hotel by the highway."

"What time was that?"

"Yesterday afternoon."

McVittie walked over to Karl and looked at his left arm. "You leavin' anything out?"

Karl shook his head. He knew there were tears in his eyes and if he blinked, they would betray him. So he focused as hard as he could on the other man's shirt.

McVittie leaned forward and placed his large hand on Karl's arm. "You sure?" McVittie looked into his eyes and started to squeeze his arm. Karl felt the tears on his cheeks and thought he'd pass out. Slowly McVittie released his grip, then nodded to his two guys, who began to muscle Karl out the door. "Chris, hang back." McVittie waited until Karl was out of earshot. "Don't use the Troyer farm. Take him to Joe Peirson's place, the one out beyond Maple Ridge, in the middle of nowhere."

Karl was put back into the van. He sat with his back to the side of the van and stretched out his legs. The stop and go of city traffic rocked him back and forth, jarring his left arm. After about fifteen minutes, the van started going faster. After another twenty minutes, the van slowed down and there were a few short stops. It was as if they were on some quiet country road. He guessed they'd headed east into the Fraser Valley. He thought he could smell manure.

The van stopped briefly, the front door opened and then they drove on and stopped again. Karl thought he'd heard a gate close. A moment later, the back doors opened, and he was ordered out of the van. The smell was overpowering. His captor held a handkerchief over his mouth.

"Move it."

Karl got down out of the van and looked around. He was too scared to worry about the smell. He was on a farm and could see pigs in a pen about twenty yards away. He looked down at his feet and realized he was standing in pig shit. The whole yard was covered in it. His captor stood still.

Karl looked across the yard and wondered if he should try and make a run for it. But it would be dark soon, and he knew he wouldn't get far with his bad arm. The door of a nearby building opened and an old bald man with several days' growth of beard came out. He smiled, revealing a mouthful of gums and four remaining yellow teeth.

"Joe, this is Karl. Boss wants you to take care of him for a few days. He can't leave your sight, and if he causes you any trouble, lock him up or bed him down with the pigs. We'd like him back in one piece though."

The old man chuckled. "Don't worry, I'll introduce him to Dolly and a few of the boars. It's almost feeding time, so I may have to chain him up for a while. It's been a while since I've had some company. Come on, young fella, let's you and I go say hi to Dolly."

Karl looked over to where the old man was pointing in the yard and saw some of the biggest hogs he'd ever seen. He figured they must have been three or four hundred pounds. They were penned in a small area and making a variety of different noises—grunting, squealing and even growling. He'd heard that hogs could be vicious animals with sharp teeth. Surely, he wasn't going to bed down with the hogs...

Chapter 20

George had a terrible night's sleep in the small bed at the manager's house. He kept tossing and turning, worrying about Davis and the gang, half expecting someone to come for him in the middle of the night.

It didn't help that Charan had told him he'd be taking him to the airport instead of Davis. Another sudden change of plan. Maybe Davis wasn't going after all. Maybe the gang had him? Maybe the gang would meet him at the airport, or even pick him up at the berry farm? Whatever it was, he didn't like it. He tried to read his book but couldn't concentrate. What was he going to do? He looked at his watch for the fourth time, it wasn't even 6:00 a.m. and it was still dark. He was exhausted and figured he may have got an hour's sleep at most. Worried about sleeping in, he reluctantly slid out of bed and made some breakfast. He waited for the kettle to boil and made some instant coffee. After breakfast he had a quick shower and dressed. He looked at himself in the small mirror. *Come on, George, pull yourself together. You can't just sit here. Take charge for once in your life.*

It was still dark at 7:15 a.m., but he decided it was time to go. He left a few clothes on the bed and left his wash bag and toothbrush in the bathroom. He grabbed his passport and the book he was reading and put them in his bag, then he left the cabin, locked the door, and headed toward the gate. Following the route of the previous afternoon, he found the phone booth and dialled his home number. The phone just rang and rang. He'd try again in ten minutes. Was no one up yet? Thelma was an early riser, and he doubted she was getting much sleep.

He looked out of the phone booth and saw someone was cycling toward him. Quickly, he turned away as the cyclist approached, picking up the phone and pretending to talk to someone. He watched the cyclist go by and was pleased when he didn't look back. Probably some labourer cycling to work somewhere nearby. *Don't panic*, he thought to himself.

He dialled his own number again and let it ring for a full minute. Again, there was no answer. He looked at the book, opened the back inside cover and found Paul Bolton's phone number. *Better than nothing.* He dialled the number. The phone rang three times. He was about to hang up.

"Paul Bolton here… Hello? Is anyone there? Hello…"

"Hello, it's George Koehle."

"George! Where the devil are you? Are you all right?"

"I'm scared. People are looking for me, you know. I want to turn myself in."

"Where are you?"

"I'm calling from a phone booth in Haney."

"Give me the number."

"Haney 6457."

"What street?"

"Hale Road, not far from Banjeeta Farm."

"How do spell that?"

"B-a-n-j-e-e-t-a."

"Okay, stay by the phone, don't move. I'll arrange for someone to get there as soon as possible."

"I can't stay here; they'll find me."

"Who'll find you?"

"Charan, Davis, the gang—"

"Charan? Who—"

"Listen, I don't have time to explain. They could be here any minute. There's a row of hedges lining the field, I'll hide there. Okay? How long will you be?"

"Someone will be there as soon as possible. Let's say 9:00 a.m. at the latest."

"That's over an hour and a half from now! Can't they get here sooner? They're probably looking for me right now."

"All right, just calm down, mate."

"How the heck am I supposed to calm down?"

"Just stay put, okay?"

"Wait. How will I know it's them?"

Bolton thought for a few seconds. "I'll tell them to bring a whistle."

"Everyone will hear that. You'll bring them straight to me."

"Well, what do you bloody well suggest?"

"I don't know. Tell them to whistle softly. And please hurry." George hung up.

He left the phone booth. He was sure the gang would soon come looking for him. He walked down Hale Road, looking for the gate. There were some cattle at the far end of the field and hedgerows as far as he could see. He climbed over the gate and headed east, about twenty yards. There wasn't much cover from the hedge, and it was too close to the gate. He walked farther until the hedge thickened out. This would be as good a place as any to hide. He took his coat off and laid it on the ground, opened his book and started reading. And then he started to laugh at himself. Here he was in the middle of some farmer's field, reading a book while waiting to be rescued. Or caught. But he wasn't scared anymore, and he didn't know why.

***

Bolton sat back in his chair, taking it all in. He called Lossan's direct line at the office and got put through to the switchboard. They said Lossan was out at a meeting and not expected back till later.

"This is an emergency."

"You can try his radio phone number; he might be in his car."

Bolton clenched his teeth. "Fine. Tell him that George Koehle phoned and wants to hand himself in. He called from a public pay phone on Hale Road in Haney. The number's Haney 6457. It's close to a farmer's field. Do you have all that?"

"Yes, I do, sir."

"I've arranged to meet him there by 9:00 a.m."

"Do you think it's wise that you go there on your own?"

"No, I bloody well don't. But what choice do I have? Tell Lossan I'll meet him in a farmer's field on the north side of the road close to the phone booth. Oh, tell him he might want to bring police dogs."

Bolton got his coat and wallet. He thought about telling someone in the office where he was going but decided to get out there as soon as he could. He drove out onto Pender Street, heading for the valley.

He was playing the boy scout again. Rushing in rather than letting the authorities sort things out. What was he thinking? He wasn't. He was on auto pilot, like the time he'd applied to join the Metropolitan Police in London. Always fascinated by fraud, he saw himself as some white knight chasing the bad guys. He never joined the police—he knew he'd have trouble with authority, always questioning why things were done this way or that. He was impatient and often took things into his own hands. It was probably why he left the boring world of audit for what he thought was the exciting world of forensic investigation. But sometimes you could have too much excitement.

There was no traffic as he drove along the side streets out of the city. At that time of the morning, most of the rush hour traffic was coming into the city. Had he made a mistake? Why had George called him? Why not his wife or Lossan? He should have stayed in his office and waited for Lossan's call.

Whether he showed up or not didn't really matter. Lossan would get the message soon enough, and if George had to wait an extra hour, it wouldn't be the end of the world. He'd call Lossan again. Then he'd stay put. He'd done his bit and look where it got him. Nothing good would come from him trying to help. He could end up in the middle of a gang.

Driving along Pitt River Road, he found a phone booth just off the main road and parked the car. It was 8:35 a.m. As he got out of the car, a woman entered the booth. He stood outside and hoped she wouldn't be long. After about three minutes, he knocked on the door and opened it.

"Excuse me, but this is an emergency."

The woman seemed annoyed. "I'll only be a minute."

Bolton took his hand off the door and let it close. If she wasn't out in thirty seconds, he'd open the door and take the phone out of her hand. He made a point of looking at his watch and he could see she was looking in his direction as she kept talking. After a minute, he pulled the door open. "I have to go," she said. She put the phone down and pushed past him as she left the booth.

Bolton phoned Lossan's direct line at Heather Street. The line was busy. He then tried his radio phone number. There was no answer, and after about twenty seconds, he got put through to the switchboard. He told the operator he was trying to reach Lossan urgently.

"He called just a few minutes ago. He said to tell you that he needed to make some arrangements, but expected to be out in Haney by about 9:30 a.m."

Bolton left the phone booth and got back into his car. He headed out to the farm. Hopefully Lossan wouldn't be late, and he wouldn't run into Davis or the gang. He pulled off the Lougheed Highway and found the turn for Hale Road. He drove down the narrow road for about a mile and saw a farm gate and then a sign for Banjeeta Farm. Within about half a mile, he noticed a phone booth on the left-hand side of the road. He pulled over, got out, and checked the number in the phone booth. It was the phone George had called him from.

He drove on until he found a farm gate, then started looking for somewhere out of the way to park his car. After about a hundred yards, he found a small lay-by on the right side of the road. He parked and walked back toward the rendezvous point he'd agreed to with George. He'd be safer walking inside the field where he wouldn't be seen from the road. After about thirty yards, the hedge thinned out and he looked to see if he could crawl through. It was a narrow gap, but he managed. Keeping close to the hedge on the inside of the field, he walked west toward the farm gate. Every now and then he could hear a car drive past along Hale Road. He was about to start whistling when he heard another car drive slowly by. And then it stopped. Bolton froze. He could hear car doors open and close. And then voices.

"He can't have gone far, he's on foot."

"He could be anywhere by now. Who knows when he left."

A moment later, two car doors closed, and the car drove off.

Bolton looked at his watch. It was 9:15 a.m. George had probably given up on him by now. And was that the gang? There might be more of them around. Any noise, even a whistle, could bring them to him. He started walking again, staying closer to the hedge. He didn't think he was too far from the gate. Hopefully George would keep his head down and not panic and try and make a run for it.

He looked through the hedge to the road as he walked, half expecting to see someone looking at him from the roadside. His progress was slow, the field was saturated after weeks of rain and had recently been plowed. His shoes and the bottom of his trousers were soaked.

Finally, he came to a gate. He must have missed George and was about to turn back when he heard a light whistle. He turned around and followed the sound, walking about ten yards before coming to a gap in the hedge. He'd passed this spot a few seconds before but hadn't noticed anything.

"Bolton? Is that you?" Bolton looked at the hedge and couldn't see anyone. "I'm up here!"

Bolton looked up. About eight feet off the ground, sitting on a branch of a tree in the middle of the hedge, was George Koehle.

"What are you doing up there?"

"I heard a car stop and then voices, so I climbed up here." George climbed down from the branch and stretched his legs. "So, what do we do now?"

"We wait. It sounds as if there's a few people looking for you, so we're better off waiting for the police. Lossan should be here soon. This tree is as good a place as any. Is there room for two?"

"I'll show you the way."

No sooner had the two of them climbed up the tree, when a car came along the road. It stopped and two doors opened. "He's around here somewhere. He couldn't have got that far."

"Charan," whispered George.

Bolton looked at George and touched his lips with his forefinger. George nodded. They heard the car drive off but stop again a few seconds later. Bolton guessed they were parked by the gate. George tried to climb a little farther up the tree.

Suddenly, Bolton heard another car coming down the road, and then another. There was screeching of tires and car doors opened and closed. He heard several voices and dogs barking. Bolton smiled.

"What are you smiling at?"

"The cavalry has arrived."

There was a lot of commotion and what sounded like arguing. Bolton heard two doors being opened and shut. Then there was silence. Within a minute two, Alsatian dogs stood barking up at them from the base of the tree, followed by their handlers and Lossan.

"You can come down now." Lossan laughed.

Bolton climbed down the tree. "What kept you?"

Lossan grinned. George took his time coming down the tree, looking warily at the dogs that were being patted by their handlers.

"Pat, this is George Koehle."

"Mr. Koehle, do you have any idea where Alan Davis is?"

"He was going to pick me up at the farm this afternoon, but he told Charan his plans changed."

"Who's Charan?"

"One of the owners of the farm I've been staying at for the last few days. Charan told me that he would take me to the airport instead."

"Which airport?"

"No idea."

"So, Davis doesn't know you're not at the farm? And he's expecting Charan to take you to the airport?"

"Yes, and I think Charan was just here looking for me a few minutes ago."

Chapter 21

Kovacs drove along the quiet country road until he saw police vehicles in the distance. He got out of his car and walked past officers with dogs and a police cruiser that held two agitated-looking men in turbans. When he reached the group of officers surrounding George Koehle, Lossan explained the situation.

Kovacs looked at Koehle and nodded toward the police vehicle holding the two men. "How well do those farm owners know Davis?"

Koehle shrugged. "Davis made out that they were old friends. I got the sense he'd helped them out in the past and they owed him something."

"Do they know where Davis is? Could he be on the farm?"

Koehle shook his head. "How the heck should I know?"

Kovacs and Lossan walked back to the cruiser and an officer helped the two men out of the vehicle. "Gentlemen, I'm Corporal Dennis Kovacs of the RCMP Security Service. We understand you know Alan Davis."

Neither of them said anything.

"Do you speak English?"

Silence.

Kovacs shook his head and stepped forward. "Okay, take 'em downtown. See if they're more responsive after a few hours in a cell. In the meantime, we'll have a look around the farm."

Suddenly, one of the men found his voice. "That won't be necessary, officer. We will be happy to cooperate. I'm Charan Sangha, and this is my brother Harman. Our father owns the Banjeeta Farm. We live here with our families."

"When was the last time you talked to Davis?"

"Last night. He said there'd been a change of plans and he asked us to take Mr. George to the airport instead … something about some people looking for him."

"Did he say who?"

"No, and I didn't ask. He said he was the one in danger, not Mr. George. I told him that we would arrange for someone to drop Mr. George off at the airport."

"Which airport?"

"Langley."

Kovacs motioned to Lossan and the two of them walked away from the group. "What if he made this up?" Kovacs said. "What if Davis is here on the farm? We need to check and have the Pitt Meadows and Abbotsford airports watched as well."

"You don't believe him?" Lossan asked.

"Thirty years of chasing scumbags will do that to you, Pat. Besides, we'd look stupid if we didn't check the farm." Kovacs took a hard look across the field to where George was standing with Bolton. "And let's take Koehle to the airport. It's our best shot at catching Davis."

Lossan waved to a couple of officers and asked them to accompany the brothers on a search of the farm, land, and buildings. The fact that they'd agreed to the search without a warrant convinced him that Davis probably wasn't there. Kovacs and Lossan walked over to George and Bolton and explained their plan.

George raised his eyebrows. "You want me to do what? I've just spent the last twenty-four hours figuring out how to escape from Davis, and now you want me to meet him at the airport?"

Kovacs shrugged. "He might not even show up. Probably out of the country by now. And given all the trouble you caused, it's the least you can do."

George turned pink and went quiet for a few minutes, but when he looked up at the other men again, he looked composed. "Fine," he said. "I'll do it."

***

Davis had a bad night. The sagging mattress didn't help. *I'm really going*, he thought. *I'm getting on that plane to Costa Rica no matter what. I can never come back. I know too much.* As he was sitting and waiting to order in the ABC restaurant next door, he looked at the people having breakfast and wondered what it must be like to lead a normal life. Not looking over your shoulder all the time, wondering what could go wrong, what was next, and who to please today? He'd changed. He'd settle for a simple life. He didn't care about money anymore. Maybe he could be a fishing guide up north or a ranch hand in the interior. *I might even find something like that down there, but I'll miss the north.*

He hadn't given much thought to how the change would affect him. He knew it'd be an adjustment and wondered how he'd settle in down there. *One month at a time*, he thought, *that's how.* Peace of mind is more important than where you live.

Davis had known gang members who'd squealed on their brothers. They'd ended up in protection, moving every few years. Never in the same place for long. The family would usually split up. If it was just the husband and wife, it was easier. But they usually lived in a small hick town that no one in their right mind would even consider. The wife would try and make a go of it for a while. But then she'd get fed up with not being able to make friends or afraid of getting too close and too settled. Kids just made it much worse. You couldn't keep moving the kids, you couldn't tell them not to make friends. Living with the knowledge that your past would one day catch up with you, always looking over your shoulder, it was no life.

He knew one guy who tried to fake his own death. Not convinced that he was dead, the gang interrogated one of his brothers, using a blow torch till he finally admitted that he hadn't drowned. They tracked him down and killed both of them. Davis was glad that he hadn't seen his family in years.

He left the motel at 11:30 a.m., wanting to get to the airport early and find a place to hide. He needed some clothes to change into so he could pass for someone who worked there. A pair of overalls and a baseball cap pulled low over his head would have to do. A block or so away was a rundown hotel that seemed to have cabs coming and going. He didn't have to wait long before a cab pulled up.

"Where to, sir?"

"Langley airport, but I need to stop and buy some clothes on the way."

"There's a mall in Langley, on the Fraser Highway on the way to the airport."

There was little traffic heading east on the highway, and they soon reached the 200th Street turnoff for Langley. The cab driver pulled into the shopping mall and parked in front of The Bay.

Davis handed him some cash. "Here's twenty bucks in case you're afraid I'll disappear. I won't be long." Then he headed for the main entrance and walked into the store. He picked up a large-size men's black overalls, a black baseball cap without a logo, a pair of size-ten sneakers and a cheap backpack. He paid cash for the clothes and backpack and put them inside his bag. As he was walking back to the cab, he passed a small hardware store and bought a small tin of dark blue paint, some cloths and a screwdriver. He was back in the cab in less than fifteen minutes.

The cab pulled up in front of the Langley airport, and Davis was surprised how small it was. It was going to be difficult to avoid being noticed. There was a bank of counters, some of which were manned. He counted fourteen people inside the terminal. Looking out to the runway, he could see some hangars at the far end. He noticed a few men outside in overalls walking back and forth. A middle-aged man dressed in a jacket and tie with a badge on his lapel that said AC Airways approached Davis.

"Can I help you, sir?"

"Yes, I'm on a private flight. Where do I check in?"

"Out the main doors on airside and head left over to the small hangar," he said, pointing outside. "You'll see a small hut where you check in."

"Thank you. Where are the washrooms?"

"Just past the restaurant, down there toward the end of the building on the left. You can't miss them."

"Thanks."

Davis headed to the washrooms and walked past a small restaurant called the Runway Café. Apart from the girl behind the counter, there were three people in the restaurant having lunch, two of whom were wearing overalls. They didn't look at him as he passed by. On the other side of the corridor was a series of offices.

Once inside the washroom, he went to a cubicle and pulled out his overalls and sneakers and the can of paint. He neatly folded his trousers and jacket and put them in the backpack along with his shoes, passport and other belongings. He opened the can of paint with the screwdriver, dipped a cloth in it and smudged different areas of his overalls and his sneakers. He used another cloth and dried the smudges, then put on his overalls and sneakers and checked himself in the mirror. He saw a storage room in the washroom and tried the door. It was locked. He used the screwdriver to open the door, and he hid the can of paint and cloth inside. He'd need to scope the place out before George got there.

Davis picked up his backpack, walked back to the airside entrance and turned right, in the direction of a large hangar. No one paid him any attention as he passed an open hangar with three light aircraft and headed toward another hangar a bit farther away. It was much bigger, with a large helicopter inside. He didn't see anyone but noticed some stairs leading to another floor, which he assumed housed offices. There was a light on. He carried on, passing the helicopter hangar. A few people working on the light aircraft looked up. One waved to him, he waved back.

It was 1:00 p.m. If George was coming, he'd be here soon. He wanted to observe him from a distance and make sure he was alone. He walked to the private aircraft hangar where he was supposed to meet Parsons. Just beyond it, he noticed the control tower. There was a small, one-storey building at the far side of the hangar with a sign that said Check-in. He'd expected Parsons would be landing shortly. There didn't appear to be anywhere to hide. Then he spotted an old fixed-wing aircraft with an open cockpit at the side of the hangar about thirty yards away. It offered a good view of the runway as well as the hangar and terminal. He walked over to the aircraft, pretending to inspect it, and looked back at the hangar to see if he was being watched. Seeing no one, he climbed onto the wing and got into the plane. He sat in the back of the four-seater aircraft and slid down the seat as far as he could while maintaining a good view of the runway and the terminal building. It was 1:20 p.m.

Davis expected George would wait until the last minute and might even stay in the terminal building and wait for him. He'd wait until Parsons's plane had arrived, then he'd go get George. He saw two men walking toward him with a dog. As they got closer, Davis realized that one of the men was blind and the dog was a guide dog. He relaxed a bit and told himself it wouldn't be much longer.

Parsons flew a Cessna Centurion six-seater that had a range of over one thousand nautical miles. It was over thirty-five hundred nautical miles to Costa Rica, and the trip would take three days and require at least four stops. They'd known each other for several years and had done business together. Nothing major, just importing minor amounts of drugs supplied by their Colombian friends. Davis expected he'd be doing more business with Parsons once he was down there on a permanent basis. But he had to get down there first.

The blind man and his friend had headed into the hangar. Parsons had yet to land. It was 1:45 p.m. and he was cutting it fine. It was time for Davis to head back to the terminal and get George. He grabbed his backpack and quickly climbed out of the aircraft. He pulled his cap down over his head and walked toward the terminal. He didn't turn his head when he walked past the hangar, even though he was no more than thirty feet from the entrance. He didn't think he'd been spotted, and he didn't look back.

As he entered the terminal, he looked around. Nothing unusual, the ten or so people he could see appeared to be going about their business. He headed to the washroom, and, as he passed the restaurant, he noticed George sitting at a table on his own. There were four other diners at another table. George glanced up but didn't seem to recognize him.

He sat down at a table next to George, who looked up again but still didn't seem to recognize him. Davis raised his cap and George's eyes widened. He pulled his cap back down and said quietly, "Wait a couple minutes, then follow me. Turn left once you're outside the terminal building and head toward the hangar. There's a small office just inside. I'll meet you there."

"What about—"

"No time for questions, George."

Davis got up and left the restaurant. As he walked through the terminal, he glanced around but nobody paid any attention. As he went through the door to the runway, he spotted Parsons's Cessna taxiing down the runway toward the hangar. He kept walking and didn't look back, keeping his cap pulled over his head and looking straight ahead. The plane came to a halt on the other side of the hangar, and the pilot turned off the engine. It about thirty yards away. He looked back; George wasn't behind him.

Davis boarded the Cessna and sat in the co-pilot's seat. He told Parsons the other passenger was on his way. They'd give him five minutes. He looked down the runway and then over to the hangar. He looked at his watch—his five minutes were up—and then out through the cockpit windshield. George wasn't coming. He told Parsons they should go.

Parsons closed the door, got back in his seat, put on his seat belt and turned on the radio. He asked the tower for permission to take off. After some static on the radio, the message came back: "Roger Zulu 140, cleared for takeoff." Parsons taxied onto the main runway and then opened the throttle. They were less than fifty yards down the runway when he noticed the two fire trucks coming toward them from the end of the runway with their red lights flashing and sirens blazing. The trucks turned across the runway and blocked their path. Parsons throttled back the engines.

"What the hell are you doing?" shouted Davis.

Parsons pointed to the end of the runway. "They've blocked the runway."

"Then turn around and take off from the other end, goddammit. Come on, let's go."

As Parsons started to taxi around, another fire truck and two police cars came driving onto the runway from behind and surrounded the small plane. There was no way out. Parsons cut the engine. "I have to let them on."

Parsons got up and opened the door. Two police officers climbed aboard and one asked for identification. Parsons showed him his pilot's licence. He was then ordered off the plane. Davis was already out of his seat.

"Alan Davis, we have a warrant for your arrest in connection with various fraudulent activities relating to Goldstate Finance. You have the right to remain silent, but anything you do say can and will be used in a court of law against you."

Davis looked at the cop, shrugged and put his hands up. He walked down the stairs and onto the tarmac steps and was told to put his hands behind his back. He noticed the blind man and his dog about thirty feet away. He realized the guy was a cop and the guide dog a police dog. The police had been there all along. The officer cuffed him. Both he and Parsons were put in separate police cars and driven off.

Kovacs and Lossan headed to the restaurant. George was still sitting in the same seat, talking to the undercover cop who'd dropped him off. He smiled at them, glad that his ordeal was over. Kovacs looked at George. "We got Davis," he said. Kovacs scanned the area for the hundredth time. Taking George Koehle to the airport had been a risk. Gang members might even be there, but Kovacs didn't catch anything suspicious on his radar.

George interrupted his thoughts. "What's going to happen to me now?"

"We'll find somewhere safe for you to stay." Lossan told George he'd arranged for Thelma to be taken to a safe house. They'd had no news of Karl and hoped that he'd headed out of town or was hiding somewhere with friends. Thelma Koehle had no idea where he'd gone and doubted he'd have gone to her sister's in northern Alberta. She thought it was more likely he'd stay with one of his friends but was worried that he had no way of contacting her.

Kovacs motioned to the cop next to George and both men stood up.

"Can I see my wife?"

"We'll see what we can arrange."

Kovacs needed to find a secure place for George until they had a chance to question him. Word would soon get out that he was still alive, and they needed to find out what, if anything, he knew about the gang. Kovacs and the other officers began to shepherd George through the airport, looking side to side as they moved toward the exit.

George suddenly stopped and turned to Kovacs. "What's going to happen to Davis?"

"He's going to a cell downtown. Isolation for now." Kovacs hoped they'd get him there without incident. Once the gang heard that Davis had been arrested, they'd try to get to him. And Kovacs needed to find a way to make Davis talk before that happened.

Chapter 22

Kovacs wasn't expecting to get much from Koehle. They had him in a safe house under guard, for now, but getting Davis to talk was critical. Even in solitary confinement the gang could find a way to get to him. The sooner he talked, the better. It wouldn't be easy, but if all else failed, Kovacs knew a way. Not exactly legal, but he'd done it before. Lossan wouldn't approve, too much by the book. But then, Kovacs didn't intend on telling him.

For now, Kovacs would question Davis at the police station. He stepped into the interview room where Davis was sitting at the table in handcuffs.

"I'm Corporal Kovacs with the RCMP Security Service. This interview is being recorded. Can you please state your name for the record?"

Davis stretched his legs in front of him and yawned. "I'm not saying anything till I've seen my lawyer."

Kovacs pursed his lips. The bastard was lawyering up before he even gave his name. "You got a lawyer we can call?"

"Len Sonowsky."

Kovacs opened the door to the room and leaned out. "Constable LaPorte, please take Mr. Davis back to his cell."

Davis got to his feet and gave Kovacs a smile as he passed him on his way out of the room. A few minutes later, LaPorte came back and peeked into the room where Kovacs was still sitting, reviewing his files. "What do you think, boss?"

Kovacs looked up. "You know Sonowsky as well as I do. He's the gang's bagman. He'll tell Davis to keep quiet and the gang will take care of him." He raised his eyebrows.

"You mean…"

"The gang'll take care of him all right."

"Why'd he call Sonowsky then?" LaPorte asked.

Kovacs dropped the paper he was reading and leaned back in his chair. "Davis is playing for time, trying to figure out his options. If McVittie believes Davis won't say anything, then he'll wait for him to be released. But not long. McVittie could already be planning how to get to him on the inside. The big question for Davis is whether he trusts McVittie. The word on the street is there's no love lost between these guys. Given that Davis hasn't dealt with Koehle, he's not in McVittie's good books."

"What do we do, boss?"

"They can bail him in forty-eight hours. We can always get an extension for another forty-eight hours, but we have to have grounds that a serious offence may have been committed. We don't have anything to hold him, unless we make something up. Harbouring a fugitive is a bit of a stretch. We need to put him in a cell with one of our own for twenty-four hours. He'll go crazy 'cause he'll know word'll get out that he's sharing a cell with a cop. We can even spread the word that Davis has done a deal."

"Is that legal?"

"I didn't hear that, Constable." *No*, he thought, *we need to smoke him out. Make him more scared of his own people than us.* "Let's see what Koehle has to say. Have him brought here. Arrange for Sonowsky to run into Koehle when he comes to meet his client. That'll stir things up a bit."

***

By the time George Koehle arrived at the Vancouver police station, Kovacs had already spoken to Sonowsky. He brought Lossan up to speed by phone and said they needed to pressure Davis.

They put Koehle in a meeting room and told him they were just waiting for Lossan to join them. George wanted to see his wife and was told that arrangements had been made for them to meet up shortly.

Len Sonowsky arrived earlier than expected and demanded to meet his client alone. Sonowsky knew he'd be given a room where he could be watched, but he also knew it was illegal to record any conversation. Kovacs wished he'd taken a lip-reading course, but it wouldn't have mattered; any such evidence wasn't admissible in a prosecution. But at least it would have given him some ideas on a possible approach.

Kovacs watched from the other side of the two-way mirror as Sonowsky joined Davis in the interview room. When the door was shut, Sonowsky put his forefinger over his lips and pointed to where he thought the camera and screen were. Sonowsky relocated his chair and motioned Davis to pull his up alongside so they could sit side by side and give Kovacs and LaPorte a good view of their backs. Sonowsky didn't say anything. All Kovacs and LaPorte could see was him writing something on a pad and passing it to Davis. Occasionally, Davis would nod, and sometimes he'd write something down and pass it back. Whenever either of them looked up and turned to face the other, the camera picked up their facial expressions. For most of their meeting, neither gave much away. After about fifteen minutes, Sonowsky stood up and knocked on the door to signal that they were ready.

Kovacs and LaPorte joined the meeting, and before Kovacs sat down, Sonowsky asked to see a copy of the arrest warrant. He spent less than a minute reviewing it and then asked why his client was in custody.

"Mr. Davis is under investigation in connection with the bankruptcy of Goldstate Finance," Kovacs said.

Sonowsky smiled and said, "As you know, Corporal, my client is neither a director or officer of Goldstate, and never has been. What evidence do you have that he has ever had anything to do with this company?"

"Let's not play games. Your client has been the mind and matter of Goldstate for some time."

"What evidence do you have other than the statement of one George Koehle? Hardly a credible witness. Isn't he behind a multi-million-dollar fraud?" Sonowsky stared across the table at Kovacs, who decided not to share the fact that his client had been a cheque signatory of Goldstate for several months. Sonowsky smirked. "So, unless you are going to charge my client, I insist that he be released immediately."

"Mr. Sonowsky, your client has advised us that he wants legal representation in order to reach an agreement with the Crown—"

Davis stood up and leaned across the table toward Kovacs, "You bastard, you're a fucking liar! You're making all this up. I never agreed to anything and you know it."

"As I said, Mr. Davis has advised us that he wants legal representation—"

"Nice try, but we're not buying it." Sonowsky put his hand on Davis's arm. "Alan, sit down. He's just trying to wind you up. It's an old trick."

"Isn't that right, Constable LaPorte?" Kovacs said. "Didn't you hear Mr. Davis say he wanted to do a deal?"

Davis looked at Sonowsky. "Len, you know it's not true. Tell McVittie this is all bullshit."

But when Kovacs looked at Sonowsky, he knew the ruse had worked. There was doubt there. And Davis knew it too. It didn't matter what he said. Sonowsky would report this to McVittie.

Sonowsky began to gather his files. "Corporal Kovacs, nice try. I think, under the circumstances, I'd like a few more minutes alone with my client."

Kovacs smiled. "Of course, just let the officer outside the door know when you're finished. As you know, Mr. Sonowsky, we have the right to keep your client in custody for up to ninety-six hours before we charge him, and that's what we intend to do."

Outside the room, LaPorte looked at Kovacs. "Boss, you never told me that Davis agreed to a deal."

"We need to rattle Davis and force his hand."

As LaPorte and Kovacs watched from the other side of the two-way mirror, Davis was still standing and was now shouting at Sonowsky. He paced back and forth, ignoring Sonowsky's efforts to calm him down. He finally sat down and held his head in his hands. Sonowsky looked through the mirror, as if to say, *You bastard, you knew what you were doing, didn't you?*

Kovacs smiled.

Just then Lossan arrived, and Kovacs brought him up to speed.

For the first time since Kovacs had met Lossan, the young Mountie did not look happy. "You lied to Davis and you lied to his lawyer. What happens when they dispute this and prove you made it up?"

"It won't come to that."

Lossan stared at Kovacs in disbelief. "How do you know?"

Kovacs had been fighting criminals all his working life and didn't need a lecture about right and wrong. Sometimes you had to act like a criminal to catch one. "Stop being a boy scout, Lossan. You can't always do things by the book."

"You've lost sight of what we're doing. When we break the law, what makes us any different from the criminals?"

"These bastards don't deserve a break. This could be one of the biggest cases we've ever had against the gang."

"And if they prove you lied, you could blow the whole thing. Get it thrown out of court."

Kovacs thought about the times he'd bent the rules before; he hadn't always got away with it, and that's why he was still only a corporal. His gut told him this time would be different. He hoped he was right. He pushed past the other man and moved closer to the two-way mirror. "Maybe I've been chasing these guys too long and took a few short cuts, but, at the end of the day, you do what it takes to get the job done."

Lossan's face was red, and he looked like he wanted to take a swing at the older cop, but he stepped back instead. "Let's take a break before either of us says anything else. We're on the same team, remember."

Kovacs kept staring through the glass, watching Davis and his lawyer talking. But he needed Lossan's help. He glanced at the young man. "How do you want to approach Koehle?"

"I called Bolton to see if he'd join us in the interview. And I arranged for Thelma Koehle to meet us here. I think George's tongue may be a bit looser once he's had a chance to talk to his wife."

Inside the interview room, Davis sat back in his chair. Sonowsky waved at the mirror, beckoning them to come in. Lossan began to walk out of the observation room when Kovacs said, "Hold up, kid. Make 'em wait a few minutes."

Lossan stopped with his hand on the door handle. "You're enjoying this, aren't you?" He was still coming to grips with what Kovacs had said, and he wanted to be away from him.

Kovacs took a deep breath. This kid was more by-the-book than he realized. "Look, Davis is between a rock and a hard place, and Sonowsky knows it. Either way, Davis is screwed, and once he realizes that, he'll deal with us. Sonowsky's probably wondering how the hell he ever got hooked up with such lowlife."

Lossan turned back to Kovacs and looked like he wanted to say something, but LaPorte walked back in and said, "Sir, they're ready for you."

Kovacs nodded and followed LaPorte back to the interview room, where Sonowsky was standing next to his client. "My client assures me that he's never discussed or agreed to any deal with you. Your claim is a complete fabrication to force him into testifying against his will."

"In that case, there doesn't appear to be anything further to discuss. We're in the process of interviewing other witnesses. We'll be bringing charges against your client shortly."

Kovacs began to leave, but Sonowsky spoke up. "You're making a big mistake, Kovacs." Sonowsky looked down at his client. "Don't worry, I'll have you out by noon tomorrow, mark my words."

As Davis left the room, accompanied by LaPorte, Sonowsky looked at Kovacs. "You've not heard the last of this."

Kovacs watched as Sonowsky was escorted by LaPorte out of the building. No doubt the lawyer would be in touch with McVittie right away and tell him what he'd heard. Kovacs returned to the room where Lossan had been watching the interview.

"Let's see what you can find out from Koehle. Mind if I sit in on it?" Kovacs asked.

"Sure. He should be here any minute," Lossan replied.

Kovacs leaned against the wall and picked something out of his teeth with the edge of his fingernail. "I was thinking," he said slowly, "of telling Davis we're moving him to Oakalla." Lossan looked up from the file he'd been reading.

"We aren't really going to move him to the pen, are we?"

Kovacs smiled to himself. If Davis heard he'd be moving to a maximum-security penitentiary that was famous for riots and hostage takings, not to mention overcrowding, small cells, and overuse of solitary confinement, he'd be stressed out. And that's exactly what Kovacs wanted. He'd been bluffing at first, but the more he thought about it, he liked the idea. Even if Davis wasn't afraid of the violence, no one wanted to be in solitary in Oakalla. That meant being confined to a cell twenty-three and a half hours a day, not speaking to anyone, not visiting the library or watching TV or doing anything with other inmates. And there were no outside windows, just a five-inch square interior window facing the corridor. "We gotta keep the pressure on," Kovacs said. "He'll crack soon enough."

Chapter 23

"Mr. McVittie, it's Sonowsky. I've just come from meeting Davis."

McVittie cradled the phone to his ear as he puffed his cigar and then set it in the ashtray on his desk. "And?"

"We gotta problem. That cop, Kovacs."

"What the fuck do you mean?"

"He says Davis wants to do a deal with the Crown. Tell them everything he knows in return for immunity."

"Davis, that lying, cheating son of a bitch. I knew I should've taken care of him."

"Davis claims he's said nothing; Kovacs is making it all up."

"What the fuck? You believe him?"

"Yes. Kovacs has nothing. He's just trying to scare Davis, make him more afraid of you than he is of the police. He's hoping you'll go after Davis so he might as well deal with the cops."

"So, this asshole Kovacs is playing a little game with us?"

"They've nothing on him and there's no way, even with George Koehle's evidence that they'll be able to hold Davis."

"And what can this son of a bitch Koehle tell them?"

"Nothing. His business was in trouble and you were kind enough to loan him money. The interest rates were a little high, but I can't see how they can trace the money to any of your other activities. Remember Koehle is the one that defrauded the bank."

"Did Davis say why he hadn't dealt with Koehle yet?"

"We didn't get into it and I don't think we should... I mean, it would be best to have this chat in person. Alone."

"You don't trust my guys?" Sonowsky was saying something, but for a moment, McVittie was quietly thinking about the empire he'd built. With men he couldn't trust. Sure, they were all scared of him—all except for Davis. He wasn't scared of anyone.

"Walter, are you still there?"

"Yeah."

"What do you want me to do?"

"Let's meet later. Usual spot, 4:00 p.m."

Davis knew too much. McVittie had to deal with him. Clearly, Kovacs had set him up. McVittie pushed his chair back from his desk and stood up. His knees were bad these days, but there was no way he was going to walk around with a cane. He grunted as he stepped around the desk. Then he headed out and over to the bar of the clubhouse, where he saw Charlie Coulson, one of the few gang members McVittie trusted. Coulson never questioned instructions, always did what he was asked to do. If he was scared of McVittie, he never let on. And he never backed down from a fight. That's why McVittie liked to use him to intimidate people and dish out punishment when it was required. McVittie liked to think his loyal lieutenant would even take a bullet for him.

"Charlie, let's you and I go for a little drive." They headed out to the parking lot and climbed into McVittie's pickup. McVittie settled into his seat and said, "Keep an eye out. See if we're being followed." Coulson leaned back in the passenger seat to get a better view and adjusted the side mirror. McVittie placed his two big hands on the steering wheel and stared hard out the windshield. "We still have our guy on the inside?"

"Roberts? Yeah, boss. But he's not on the beat anymore, he's on administrative duties. Been accused of tampering with evidence."

"Davis is being held downtown. It seems they think he can help them with this Koehle matter."

"He won't say anything, boss. You know Davis."

"Maybe, but I need Roberts to find out when and where they're going to move him. If they keep him downtown for a few nights, I want to know."

As McVittie pulled out of the clubhouse driveway, he looked up and down the street and saw a few parked cars but couldn't see anyone in them.

"Call Roberts and set up a meeting for tonight, at Brighton Park, down by the PNE. Tell him 8:00 p.m." McVittie glanced in his mirror. "Anyone following us?"

"I haven't seen a soul."

McVittie pulled over at the corner of Commercial and First to let Coulson out. "I'll see you tonight, Charlie, and don't be late."

"Got it, boss, see you later."

McVittie was already driving away, his mind on Davis, who he figured was probably being kept in solitary. McVittie frowned. He needed to move quickly, and he'd probably only get one chance. And Davis would be expecting it. The best chance was where there'd be a lot of prisoners. Maybe the showers, or when he was let out to exercise, probably a walk in the prisoners' yard. It wouldn't take long.

***

Half an hour later, McVittie pulled into the Peirson property. It was even filthier than he remembered. Peirson had been on his own ever since his mother died ten years ago. He rarely washed, shaved once a week, only had a few teeth, and smelled as bad as his pigs. McVittie shook his head. He remembered the time Peirson told him he talked to his pigs. Claimed that if you didn't treat them right, pigs could be downright vicious and could bite something fierce. Joe was a weird guy, but he was useful.

When McVittie got to the rundown trailer surrounded by broken-down cars and other rusted machinery, Joe Peirson opened the trailer door before he had even stopped the truck. McVittie slid down from his seat and headed toward the trailer.

"Walter McVittie. Haven't seen you in ages."

"Thought I'd come and see how your guest was doing." McVittie couldn't help glancing around him and frowning. The smell was almost unbearable.

"Lippy little bugger. Don't know where these kids get their attitude. No respect these days. He got me so mad, had to chain him up in the barn."

McVittie laughed. "Did it work?"

"Dunno. I been inside most of the time."

"Have you seen Davis?"

"He was out here a while ago, said he might need my help, something about a friend he wanted to hide for a while."

"Did he say who?"

"No, and the guy never showed up."

"All right. Take me to the kid."

Joe led him to one of the old sties. Inside, Karl was sprawled on a stone floor in leg irons, with one hand handcuffed above his head to the wall. The other arm was laying awkwardly across his leg. His eyes were closed.

"Take the chains off. I need to talk to him."

Joe undid the chains and stood up. Karl's arm fell down by his side but otherwise he didn't move. Joe gave him a swift kick in the side, and Karl groaned, but his eyes stayed closed. McVittie leaned in to take a closer look. Karl's his face was sweaty and his skin had a yellow tint. And he smelled. The kid had soiled his pants.

McVittie wrinkled his nose and stepped back. "Get some water." *Shit. This is all I need.*

When Joe came back with the water, McVittie motioned toward Karl. "Give him some." Joe bent down and lowered the mug to Karl's mouth, but the kid's lips barely opened. His eyelids fluttered when Joe dribbled cold water on his chin and neck.

McVittie looked over Joe's shoulder and pursed his lips. "You awake, kid?" Karl moved his head slightly, but he was still out of it. "Goddammit," McVittie muttered. He couldn't call an ambulance. Not to the farm. He'd call Charlie and have him come and drop him off at a nearby hospital. Karl wasn't going to be much use to anyone in this state. Then McVittie got an idea. "Joe, you got a camera?"

"Yeah, one of them Polaroid things. You know the instant ones."

"Get it."

When Joe returned with the camera, McVittie instructed him to take a head shot. Joe pressed a button and a few seconds later a photo came out of the front of the camera. McVittie looked at the picture. A bit dark, but his dad would be able to recognize him, even in this state. "Take one more, and this time, sit on the ground when you take it."

The photo was a little better.

"What do you think, son? Will your old man recognize you?" He laughed and walked back to his truck. "Keep giving him water, and food if he'll take it. Don't want him dying, do we? I'll arrange for Charlie to come by and take him to a hospital." McVittie put the photos in his pocket and looked at his watch. There was still a lot to do.

Chapter 24

George had been taken to a safe house in a remote part of Langley. He was anxious to see his wife. He didn't like being on his own; it gave him too much time to think. He lay down on his bed and stared at the ceiling. He'd really screwed things up.

He rolled over and stared out the window. What would become of his company? The investors? He sighed. He could pretend he wasn't sure, but he knew what would happen. The bank would get the assets back and sell them for whatever they could get for them. The investors would lose everything. He'd be on the hook for the bank debt and probably lose the house. Maybe even go bankrupt personally.

What would happen to Thelma and Karl? He'd been a poor husband and a lousy father. He'd certainly be thrown out of the church. Shunned by the church community. Thelma might be asked to leave too. If she stayed, their relationship would be over—she and Karl would have to shun him too. But that would mean she'd be shunned as well. Marriage breakups were not tolerated.

George sat up. The church meant so much to her. Where was it all going to end? One thing he was good at was feeling sorry for himself. If this had taught him anything, it was that self-pity was a weakness. He needed to stand up and face the consequences, and this was just the start. Family was more important to him than anything, especially the business. He just hoped it wasn't too late to save his marriage and keep his family together.

***

When they finally brought George to the Vancouver police station, Thelma was already there, looking paler than usual, her small hands wrapped around a Styrofoam cup, her eyes blank. She stared at him as he walked into the small interview room. There was so much he wanted to say. He sat across from her, set his hands on the table, close enough that she could have taken them if she wanted to. Instead, she looked down, lifted the cup of cold tea and took a sip. When the officer who'd brought him there left the room, shutting the door behind him, George leaned toward her. "Thelma ... I—"

"No one has heard from Karl. I'm really worried."

"Don't worry, Thelma, he'll be fine. Probably staying with a friend somewhere out of sight."

"Corporal Kovacs said they're still looking for him," she said, still looking down.

George waited until she looked up. "Thelma—"

"George, I want the truth. I understand the police are proposing some sort of deal, a suspended sentence and protection for all of us. Why on earth would we need protection? What is going on?" Thelma knew about the gang. She wanted to know if he was still lying.

George told her about hiding at the berry farm, and how the police seemed more interested in the gang than in what he'd been doing.

"He called me," Thelma said softly.

For a moment, George didn't know what she was talking about.

"Karl. He told me this ... *gang* was following us. That we were in danger." She'd been fidgeting with the Styrofoam cup, staring down at it. "And now he's missing." George heard a crack in her voice and thought she might be crying. But when she looked up, her eyes were dry. Her mouth was a straight line of resolve. "How could you do this? How could bring this down upon our family?" George opened his mouth and closed it again. She looked at the two-way glass on one side of the room, her eyes fluttering briefly. "How long have you been involved with these people?"

"It's only in the last few months that I realized who these people were. When Davis showed up, it was just to help with a loan. He knew people that had money." George hated the sound of his voice.

"Davis showed up almost three years ago. In all that time you never once thought to tell me. What if they've got Karl?"

"It won't come to that. Trust me."

"Trust you?" There was no quiver in her voice now. "How can I ever trust you again? You've put our lives at risk—our son's life—and never once thought about it."

There was a knock on the door. An officer entered. "I can take you back to the safe house, ma'am."

Thelma stood up. "I'd rather wait here. In case there's any news about Karl." The officer nodded and directed her to step out of the room. As she passed by George, he stood up and reached for her. "Don't touch me!" She pulled her arm away. "Don't come anywhere near me. If anything happens to Karl, I'll never forgive you." She followed the officer out without looking back.

George watched her walk away and stood there staring until Lossan came to fetch him. Lossan agreed that Kovacs would conduct the interview. "Take a seat," Kovacs said. "You're not being charged at this time. I'm confirming that you're here of your own free will."

George sat down and nodded. "Yeah. My own free will," he muttered.

Kovacs asked him to give them a brief history of the company and Alan Davis's role. And for the next hour, George explained how he had relied on investments from private individuals who were members of his wife's church. How he missed payments on the bank's debt and on the mortgages of the Hawaiian properties. And how one of the business brokers he'd turned to suggested Alan Davis might be able to help.

George was starting to relax. There was something cathartic in talking about everything that had happened. It was like a therapy session. He was about to ask for a coffee when Lossan leaned over and whispered something to Kovacs and then left the room. George sat up again. He was going to ask what this was about, but Lossan returned quickly and again whispered something to Kovacs, who then looked at George.

"Karl? Is this about my son? Have you found Karl?" George looked back and forth between the men.

Kovacs gave him a hard look and waited a moment before answering. "No. This is about the interview. We'd like Mr. Bolton to sit in. You okay with that?"

George was so relieved he would've agreed to anything. "Fine. That's fine."

A moment later, Bolton joined Lossan at the table with George. Kovacs stood near the wall, his arms crossed, and listened to Lossan reread part of George's earlier statement leading up to the company's financial troubles.

George began to explain how hard it had been for him, trying to keep his business afloat, trying to keep investors happy.

"Yeah, we've heard all this." Kovacs pushed himself off the wall and stepped forward, his dark eyes flashing. "What we want to know is how Davis is involved."

George swallowed. "Can I ... have something to drink. Maybe—"

"You'll get a drink when we're done." Kovacs was gripping the back of Lossan's chair, and George felt suddenly relieved he wasn't alone with the man.

"Okay ... well, after Davis arranged for the loan, he took on a more active role in the day-to-day management of the business." George glanced up and all three men were staring at him, Lossan with a pen poised over his yellow legal pad. George cleared his throat. "Funds were deposited into the Goldstate bank accounts and then transferred out again … from a variety of different numbered companies' bank accounts. Davis started to review all the cheques and transfers, and he always made sure we had funds, you know, to cover payroll and interest."

"And where did he tell you the money came from?" Lossan asked.

"He didn't." George leaned back in his chair. "I swear, he didn't," he repeated quietly. "And I … I just let it go. You know, 'cause it was easy that way."

Bolton looked at Lossan as though asking for permission, and the big officer smiled and nodded. Bolton turned his blue eyes on George. "Did anyone keep a record of the deposits and payments from these numbered companies?"

"We started to." George looked hopeful. Perhaps he wasn't entirely at fault. "The monthly deposits were always close to the amounts they withdrew."

"Did your accountants ever ask who was behind the money?" Bolton asked.

"We just told them it was a new investor. But, you know, after a while they knew something was wrong. Our situation never improved. Then that blasted Davis made me open a new bank account with another bank in the company's name. He wanted to advance funds from that account rather than our BC bank."

Bolton was leaning forward now, like wolf on the hunt. "Did you have any idea who was behind this money?"

"I thought it was this guy Davis knew. He never told me his name. But after a while I…" George looked down at his hands. They looked so old.

"Yeah?" Kovacs prompted.

George looked up again. "I realized they were running money through the business. I never saw the bank statements but … I did approve and sign all the transfers."

"How much money came in and out of the account?"

"The amounts varied, but at one point it was over $500,000 a month."

Bolton paused for a few seconds to let it sink in and then looked at both Lossan and Kovacs, as if to announce an important question. "Where are the company's records?"

George told them the monthly statements went to the office in Burnaby at first. Then Davis wanted to use another mailing address. George never saw the statements after that. But he'd signed a change of address for the bank. "It was for a mailbox in Burnaby, an address on Hastings Street."

"What about all the other company records? We couldn't find anything."

"Davis told me to shut down the office and get rid of all the records. So I, you know, destroyed everything."

Kovacs was hanging over the other two men on his side of the table. "Why did you transfer all those properties to your investors?"

"To protect them." George heard his voice crack. "You see, the investors are members of our church. For many of them, it was their life's savings. And they were mostly retired, and some are friends." He looked around at them all with desperate eyes. He needed them to understand. He wasn't a bad person.

"And if your wife found out, she'd kill you," Kovacs said.

George's mouth was dry. He wished they'd give him some water. "Davis told me they were arranging to put some money in, but it never happened. I think he believed we had more time. But he didn't know that I was going to transfer all those properties."

"What do you mean he didn't know?"

"It was my lawyer's idea. Steiner said we couldn't afford to wait, and that once the bank took over, they'd liquidate the assets, and the investors would be left with nothing. We didn't tell Davis what we planned to do, and when it was clear at the end—when the bank called the loan—that Davis wouldn't be putting any more money in, well ... we just did it."

"What was Davis's reaction when he discovered what you'd done?" Kovacs asked.

"He went crazy. He said it was stupid and that the bank would be even more determined to find out what was really going on."

Kovacs was leaning against the wall again, looking shrewd. "What happened then?"

"I think he was more afraid of what his boss might do. The last thing he wanted was the police investigating the company. He left me up at his place in the Cariboo, came back to the coast to find out what was happening. That's when he discovered that the police had raided the offices. When he came back up north, he was different. He was in big trouble with his boss, I could tell. His boss told him to deal with me or he would."

"Did you think he meant kill you?"

"At first. I was sure he was going to kill me up at the cabin, or somewhere in the bush. Then he seemed to calm down a bit. He said he'd pretend he buried me somewhere in the bush. I think he had enough of the gang and wanted out."

"You believed him?"

George shrugged. "I don't know. But when he changed plans and moved me to the blueberry farm instead of that pig farm, I figured he had a change of heart and decided to kill me after all or lead the gang to me."

"Did you ever meet anyone else, or hear any other names?"

"He mentioned his boss's name once. A guy named McVittie. And some farm out in the valley he planned to move me to. Some sort of hiding place. A hog farm owned by some friends of the gang."

Kovacs decided to have a break and told George they may need to talk to him again. They needed to focus on Davis. George was taken back to his minder.

Kovacs looked at Lossan and Bolton. "You believe him?"

Lossan spoke first. "I can't see why he would lie at this point. He knows he needs to cooperate."

"I agree," said Bolton. "It's a bit late in the day to make up stories. Besides, I don't think George has the brainpower to make something up. He got in over his head, he needed to keep the business afloat and made the mistake of going to the wrong people."

"Are we likely to learn much more about the gang from him?" asked Lossan.

Kovacs grunted. "We need to focus on Davis."

Lossan leaned back in his chair and rubbed his chin. "What would I do if I were Davis?"

Kovacs shrugged. "He's a dead man if he gets released and he's a dead man if he stays inside. If Koehle's right and Davis wants out of the gang, then he'll make a deal."

They decided to call it a day. Kovacs knew he needed to keep unsettling Davis. Move him to another prison, put him in solitary, make him realize that the longer he was in custody, the more likely McVittie would be to arrange for someone to go after him while he was inside. He'd break soon enough.

***

At 8:00 p.m., a guard went to Davis's cell and told him he was being moved that night but wouldn't tell him where. Davis assumed they'd keep him in protective custody. But why move him now? His only option was to reach a deal with Kovacs. Once he'd made that decision, there'd be no going back.

Davis thought about *No Way Out*, the book he'd read recently. The only way out for that gang member was to become a police informant. He'd eventually testified against his gang, sending many of them to prison. But his life changed forever in ways he could never have imagined. He had two police handlers. He was fitted with a wire, given cash and told to buy drugs from known dealers. He was told to get a gun. And they watched his every move.

Davis lay on his cot and stared at the bars around him. Was that the life he wanted? Acting as a double agent? Always watching his back. Trusting no one. Always exposed, in danger.

In the book, the biker had to sit through meetings about there being a rat in the gang. He'd often have to stop his car on the way home to throw up. Keeping all his stories straight made the stress unbearable. In the morning, he'd assume one character, then he'd change and take on a different persona with someone else that he'd met on the street or in the gym. He found it hard to live with the cobweb of lies he'd developed. His heart started to race, and three or four times a day he'd feel a jolt, like someone he couldn't see had just given him a shake. He ended up wearing a heart monitor. Lying became second nature. It was like he was on a perpetual roller coaster fuelled by speed and steroids, and it was getting faster. Finally, he was confronted about being a rat and had to bluff his way out. The guy that confronted him was an old friend and they'd joined the club at the same time. He went home realizing he'd been lucky not to have been killed by one of his closest friends. He contacted his handlers and they pulled him out the next day. He ended up in witness protection, the realm of the unknown. He never knew if he'd be walking down the street one day and bump into the wrong person and have it all end there. And he had to cut all his ties with everyone he'd known before. He lost his friends and family, and his identity. But he'd survived.

Davis decided to wait until the morning before asking to speak to Kovacs. Without him, the police didn't have anything. His years with the gang meant a lot of secrets, a lot of names, a lot of illegal businesses, and a lot of contacts with the Mexicans, the Colombians, and the Vancouver longshoremen.

He would need a good lawyer. Someone who'd prosecuted and defended serious criminals. He started to list the names in his head. There weren't too many. Few good lawyers acted for gangs. It didn't help their reputation with the Crown. But the Crown could pull some strings, given the information he had. Even Kovacs would be shocked by what he could tell them.

At 10:00 p.m., Davis arrived at Oakalla Prison.

***

McVittie arrived at Brighton Park early. There were no cars in the parking lot. It was evening and, apart from the distant overhead lights of the nearby docks, there was little light. He parked at the end of the lot, close to the trees. He still had fifteen minutes before he was supposed to meet Coulson. After a few minutes, a motor bike drove into the lot. He recognized Charlie Coulson's engine. It needed a new exhaust. Coulson flashed his lights, and he rode his bike over to McVittie's truck. He stopped his bike, turned off the engine, stood it up on its stand, took off his helmet and laid it on the bike. McVittie got out of the car and walked to the trees. The biker followed him.

"Is that rat Roberts coming?" McVittie asked. He liked having the cop on his payroll, but he didn't like the man himself. He was still a cop after all.

"Yeah, boss, he didn't want to at first. But I told him he couldn't afford to miss this meeting."

McVittie had taken a risk and it paid off. Getting a cop on their side meant inside information and even evidence that occasionally disappeared. But it wasn't always easy to find a cop willing to do the dirty work. Lucky for McVittie, Roberts had a little brother who happened to deal. When he couldn't pay McVittie what was owed, Roberts had incentive to help the gang out. In return, McVittie let his brother live. And a relationship was born.

The headlights of a car entering the lot shone in their direction. The driver parked at the entrance but left the lights and engine on.

"That him?" McVittie asked.

The driver turned off his lights and engine. Coulson walked toward the car and when he was about ten yards away, the driver got out. The cop was tall and skinny and looked like a bag of nerves, glancing from side to side as he approached them. "What's this about? I told you no more jobs. I'm already under investigation."

"I heard," Coulson said. "You gotta be more careful. We wouldn't want to lose you now, would we? Follow me."

McVittie stayed in the shadows, and as they got nearer, he said, "That's close enough."

Roberts stopped. "I'd like to know who I'm dealing with. Step into the light."

McVittie had no time for cops, especially bent ones. Not that Roberts was necessarily bent. Just weak and vulnerable. "I don't think so," he said. "A good friend of mine, Alan Davis, is being held downtown. You're gonna be our eyes and ears. If he's moved, you're gonna tell us. If he has visitors, you're gonna tell us. If he goes to the toilet, you're gonna fuckin' tell us."

Roberts gritted his teeth. He'd had enough of this shit. No brother was worth what he'd been going through for the past few years. He didn't even know where his brother was. "What if I say no?"

McVittie tilted his head. "That wouldn't be too smart. How's your kid? Little Danny must be what, five years old now?"

Roberts took a step forward with both fists clenched, but Coulson stood in his way and held up his arms.

"We're done here," McVittie said. "You got your instructions, now off you go, home to your family, there's a good lad."

Roberts was shaking with anger, but he turned and headed back to his car, got in and drove out of the parking lot.

"What's next, boss?"

"I'll tell Sonowsky to pay a visit to Davis. Reinforce the message. My guess is he'll keep quiet, but those bastard pigs might try and soften him up, tempt him. Move him to another prison. They'll keep a close eye on him, but even prisoners need exercise."

Chapter 25

Davis spent a bad night in a noisy holding cell in Oakalla. Lights were kept on twenty-four hours a day there, and even though they dimmed them at night, it was nearly impossible to sleep. He finally dozed off around four in the morning and was awakened before 7:00 a.m. by a guard banging on the door, telling him he would be moved in ten minutes. Davis jumped off the bench and called to the guard, who was already walking away. "Hey! I wanna talk to Kovacs." The guard ignored him.

Davis was escorted through an open area of the almost-seventy-year-old prison. On his left was a high fence. He knew that somewhere out there was the old prison cemetery. The inmates dug the graves, maintained the site and made the coffins and grave markers. If an inmate's body wasn't claimed by the family, he was buried in Boot Hill. Davis looked to the other side, where another high fence separated him from prisoners walking around the compound. He kept his head down, but he could feel their eyes on him. He was led through two locked gates controlled by guards and then into a room that had benches and showers. There were a set of civilian clothes on the bench and a towel.

"You got ten minutes to shower and change."

Davis didn't move. "Where am I going?"

The guard crossed his arms and stared at the wall. Davis wanted to punch him. But that would not be a good start. Instead, he got undressed and walked into the showers. He'd find out soon enough what Kovacs was planning. It felt good to have a shower and put on the clean white shirt, dark pants and brown slip-on shoes. There was no belt. When he was ready, the guard handed him a baseball cap and a bag to stick his dirty clothes in. "Pull the cap down over your head."

They went back through two sets of locked doors, but then they changed direction and headed back the way they brought him into the prison the previous evening. They came to a courtyard where a dark van was parked. Lossan stepped out of the vehicle along with a uniformed Mountie. "I hope you had a good sleep; we've got a busy day planned. Hopefully you'll be a little more talkative today."

Davis knew he was out of options, and, sooner or later, he had to either cut a deal with them or they'd release him. He wasn't sure how much longer he'd have to stay in the noisy holding cell. How was he supposed to sleep, let alone think? Maybe that was Kovacs's plan all along.

The dark blue Econoline had tinted windows and the drive from Oakalla to Heather Street through rush hour traffic was slow. Davis wondered if McVittie knew where he was. Word would get out soon enough. Eventually, they went through a manned gate and parked in the back of the Heather Street building. Maybe these guys figured there were too many loose lips downtown.

Lossan led him through a back door, and they caught the elevator to the third floor, then entered a large boardroom. Kovacs was already there, but Davis didn't recognize the others: a white-haired, bearded fat guy, a bald guy with one eye that looked freaky and a middle-aged guy with a mustache and glasses.

The man with the mustache looked up when Davis walked in. "Mr. Davis. I'm Inspector Hatley of the RCMP Commercial Crime Division." Davis just stared at him. "I'll keep this simple. We have the authority to offer you a deal. Your lawyer will advise you on whether it's enforceable. If, on the other hand, you're not prepared to cooperate, then you're free to go." Davis prayed his lawyer wasn't the freaky-eyed bald guy.

Hatley cleared his throat and gestured across the table toward the bearded man. "This is Douglas McDonald, the regional gang prosecutor." Hatley nodded toward the bald man with the weird eye. "And this is your lawyer, Richard Peek."

Davis clenched his jaw. He could feel the rage that had been building for the past few days coming to a head. "You've got it all figured out, haven't you? How do I know you guys aren't going to screw me?"

The bald guy looked at him with one good eye. "That's where I come in." Peek looked at the rest of them and said, "Gentlemen, could you give us a few minutes."

Everyone else left the room. Peek gestured to an empty chair across from him and Davis sat down. "I've acted for the Crown and the defence in a variety of BC criminal cases for over thirty years. There are no guarantees. Any deal will depend on the value of your testimony. Once I have an idea of what you know, I can tell you the likelihood of a deal. Everything you tell me is protected by solicitor–client privilege. If you want someone else, they can arrange it."

"What are the prospects of being relocated outside of Canada?"

"Unlikely. I'm only aware of two cases, both out of Montreal, where the witnesses were relocated to the United States and managed by the FBI."

"How many times have you acted for the defendant?"

"More than twenty."

"What about my family?"

"You'd all be relocated together. But I wasn't aware you had family."

Davis scowled. The odds of his ex-wife and daughter wanting to get back with him were remote. But he wasn't going to let his screw-up come back on them. "We split years ago. We have a twelve-year-old daughter. I haven't seen either of them in years. I doubt the gang know where they are, but they could find them... I want to know they're safe."

"We can put it on the table."

Davis wanted to scream. This asshole was talking about his wife and daughter like they were an afterthought. He stared at him and noticed that his left eye didn't move at all. Then he realized it was a glass eye. He took a breath and looked at his lawyer. "Where do we start?"

"Start with the big picture: how long you've been involved with the gang, what you did, who you dealt with, and we'll go from there."

Hmm. No bullshit. Maybe this guy was all right. "What's wrong with your eye?"

"A freak accident playing basketball in college. Two of us went for the ball, and his finger caught the corner of my eye and severed my optic nerve. The loss of vision was permanent." Peek had told this story a hundred times, and he recited it that way. What he left out were the years it had taken to adapt. How he now saw things from a long way off. After years of adjustment, he'd found perspective. And he'd learned how to draw people in. It had taken a long time, but he was no longer angry. The accident ceased to define him. "Let's get started, shall we?"

Davis told his story. Peek sat back and listened, occasionally making a few notes. After about thirty minutes, he'd heard enough. "It's time to deal," he said.

Chapter 26

Kovacs had some time left before the deadline expired to charge or release Davis. He decided he was going to apply for an order extending it. He was about to pick up the phone but was interrupted by a young Mountie knocking on his door. "Corporal, a Constable Roberts from Vancouver PD needs to speak to you right away. It's about the Davis case."

Kovacs leaned back thoughtfully. Then he picked up the phone again and asked for the Vancouver police. A quick conversation told him what he wanted to know. Roberts was on desk duty pending allegations about connections with gang members, threats and witness tampering. Kovacs smiled and asked to be transferred to Roberts directly.

"Hello, Roberts here."

"Yeah, this is Corporal Kovacs with the RCMP Security Service."

"Corporal Kovacs?"

"That's what I said."

"Yeah, um, I need to talk to you. It's about the Davis case. And Walter McVittie."

"Go on."

"First I need to know my family will be protected."

Kovacs wasn't in the mood to play games, but this guy might actually have something useful. And he was scared. Kovacs knew how to use that to his advantage. He took a risk. "Listen, Roberts, I know all about you and McVittie."

Silence. Kovacs was about to try another tack when Roberts broke and everything came out. He told Kovacs about his meeting the night before with Charlie Coulson and Walter McVittie. And that McVittie was going to go after Davis and knew he was being held downtown.

Kovacs had to play this just right. Keep this guy desperate. "What do you want me to do about it?"

"You have to help me." Kovacs thought Roberts might be crying on the other end of the line. "McVittie's threatened my family and he means business. He's expecting to hear from me. He wants to know if you move Davis, and if so, when and where. We need to trap him."

"My focus is Davis."

"Well, it should be McVittie. You need to take him off the streets before he gets to my fam—I mean Davis."

Kovacs sat back in his chair. "I'll call you back if I need you." He hung up. Roberts might be telling the truth; on the other hand, it could be a trap.

***

Kovacs returned to the smaller boardroom with McDonald, Lossan and LaPorte and brought them up to speed on the conversation he'd had with Roberts. He told them there was no way they could trust Roberts based on what he'd heard. They all agreed. Kovacs decided to call Roberts back and tell him they'd be in touch, knowing all the time they wouldn't be using him.

There was a knock on the door and an officer advised them that Peek was ready to meet. They followed Kovacs back into the large boardroom. Peek waited for them all to sit down and then looked up at McDonald. "I've had a chance to talk to my client. He's prepared to cooperate and testify, subject to getting various assurances about freedom from prosecution, witness protection, a new identity, relocation and compensation."

McDonald looked stern. "You know the drill as well as anybody. We can only agree once we know the extent and value of the information your client can give us."

"Once you've heard what I've heard, I don't think you'll have any problem. Mr. Davis, is it okay if I speak on your behalf?" Davis nodded.

Kovacs looked up and then across at Davis. "Mr. Peek, please continue."

As Kovacs listened to the lawyer, he was surprised at the extent of the gang's business empire. Importation and distribution of drugs from Mexico and Colombia, land development, construction, mortgage financing, payday loans, travel agencies, pubs and cabarets. While Peek was reading from notes, Lossan was watching Davis. He sat there showing no reaction. Kovacs on the other hand seemed surprised, especially when he heard that, according to Davis, they had an extensive network of individuals involved in drug importation, distribution and trafficking, which included management at the Vancouver Port Authority, longshoremen at the port and senior management at the liquor distribution branch.

According to Davis, the drugs business accounted for over ninety per cent of the cash being generated and the other businesses were used to launder the money. Lossan wondered how Davis found the time to manage all these businesses, and where the money ended up. It was hard to understand why he was only the number two guy in the organization. McVittie's reputation was that of a thug and hard man, and it was doubtful he was the brains behind this empire. Maybe Davis was the number one after all. He hated to admit it, but Lossan was developing a growing admiration for Davis's business skills. He doubted Kovacs shared that admiration.

McDonald asked Peek how involved Davis was in the business ventures. Peek explained that his client's advice was sought on business opportunities, but he never directly benefitted from any of the business ventures other than his annual modest compensation. He was never knowingly an owner of any of the business ventures, and his role was primarily to identify and acquire new businesses, oversee management of the businesses, and manage the money. Ultimately, the monies went into one account controlled by McVittie, who was solely responsible for its distribution.

McDonald stated that they were only able to offer a deal on the condition that Davis was not a major beneficiary of any of the proceeds of crime. "In the event it's subsequently proven that he was in fact a beneficiary, any agreement would be invalid unless signed off by the Director of Public Prosecutions."

Peek looked at Davis, who nodded.

"Can we be assured your client has never been involved in the commissioning of a capital offence?"

Davis nodded again.

McDonald scratched his white beard and sat back in his chair, his small blue eyes fixed on Davis. "We'll want your testimony against gang members and any other parties involved, details and location of assets, and names and addresses of individuals who profited from various activities." Davis nodded. "In return, you'll be released from prosecution and will receive witness relocation and protection within Canada and a monthly living allowance for up to ten years, subject to ongoing cooperation."

Davis winced when he heard ten years and ongoing cooperation. He wanted this thing to end, and it was only just starting. He wasn't looking forward to the weeks and weeks of examination and testimony, not to mention the isolation and protection he'd be subjected to during trial. He was beginning to have second thoughts.

When McDonald asked for further disclosure from Peek's client, Davis stood up, but Peek rescued him by putting a hand on his arm. "Well, I'm afraid that's all you're going to get. If that's not enough, I don't know what is."

Davis never let anyone touch him. But, for some reason, he wasn't bothered when Peek did it. He sat down.

Kovacs stood up and signalled to McDonald. "Gentlemen, we'll be back shortly."

The group left Davis and Peek and headed to a smaller boardroom. Before they even sat down, Kovacs addressed McDonald. "Doug, you know we have more than enough, and this could prove to be one of the best chances we'll ever have to go after McVittie and the criminals at the Port. Let's not give Davis a chance to reconsider."

"Davis isn't going to change his mind. He knows the alternative," McDonald said.

Kovacs clenched his jaw. "Davis doesn't like getting jerked around, and Peek is no amateur; he's told Davis there's enough on the table for a deal. Let's not fuck around, let's get this done."

"Okay, okay," said McDonald.

They returned to the meeting room and McDonald told Peek they were prepared to deal. Davis would return to Oakalla, where he'd remain in solitary until they made arrangements for more suitable and secure accommodation. He wouldn't be returned to the holding cell but instead to a private wing under an assumed name. And in the meantime, he'd be expected to tell them everything he knew about Walter McVittie and the gang business.

***

Over the next two days, Davis provided an extensive history of his activities since he joined the gang. He provided a list of gang members, associates and contacts responsible for the importation of illegal substances and details of all the other business activities. Davis estimated that, over the last three years alone, more than fifty thousand kilograms of drugs and related products passed through the local network and that tens of millions of dollars were funnelled through some fifteen different businesses owned by the gang.

Kovacs questioned Davis on his recollection of events, which appeared to be too good to be true. He told them that he had an almost photographic memory and had kept detailed records that he'd hidden in his cabin up north. Lossan was taking down so many notes Kovacs thought it was a wonder the young Mountie's hand didn't cramp up.

They were about to break for lunch when a knock at the door interrupted them. "This came for you, sir," said a Mountie, handing Kovacs an envelope marked Urgent. Kovacs set his coffee down and opened the envelope upside down so the photo inside slid out. He turned it over and squinted at the dark, blurry image. He could barely make out a young man half lying down, looking in pretty bad shape. Kovacs sighed. He set the Polaroid on the table and pushed it into the middle. "You recognize this person?" he asked Davis.

Everyone leaned forward to get a better look. "Looks like Karl Koehle," Davis said.

"What do you thinks happened to him?" Kovacs asked.

Davis picked the photo up. "My guess is that McVittie has the kid, and this is a message to you. He thinks he can bargain. Karl's life for mine."

"Any idea where Karl is?"

"He could be anywhere. My guess would be the Peirson farm."

"Why not the Troyer farm?"

"That's the first place they'd expect you to look. Didn't you guys raid Fred's farm a few years back? No, if I were hiding him, I'd use the Peirson farm, it's in the back of beyond, one road in and one road out. Joe Peirson's a friend of the gang, but that's all. The gang stores stuff there from time to time. He's a bit simple, not a gang member. McVittie probably had Joe scare the life out of him already. And people get scared just looking at Joe. If he's not at the farm, then my guess is you'll find his body in a garbage dump in some back alley."

Kovacs looked at LaPorte, who nodded. "I'll get a team ready, sir." He left quickly.

McDonald turned to Kovacs and quietly suggested that he arrange to apply for warrants for the arrest of five members of the gang. Kovacs nodded and McDonald got up and left the room.

Chapter 27

McVittie decided to lay low at a cabin at Cultus Lake, about ninety minutes' drive east of the city. The place would be quiet at this time of year. When he pulled up in the evening, there were no lights on in any of the nearby cabins. The place had been closed for winter. He parked his car at the back of the cabin and took his time sliding out of the truck. The cold made his joints ache even worse than usual. The last thing he needed was a fall on the slippery driveway.

When he got inside, he called Coulson. No answer. He wanted an update. Last he'd heard, there was no point in taking Karl Koehle to the hospital. Which meant the kid's body must have been stinking up Coulson's car all day until it was dark enough to dump it. That's probably where Coulson was now.

McVittie dropped the truck keys on the counter and rubbed his hands together. He could see his breath in the air, but he was too tired to start a fire, and the goddam cabin had no heat. Why the hell hadn't he thought of that? He sank onto the couch, picked up his left leg with a grimace and set it on the stool in front of him. Then he pulled a wool blanket over the leg and closed his eyes. After a moment, he placed a hand on his chest and felt the letter in his pocket. He'd taken to carrying it around lately. *I don't have a lot of time*, he thought, *and there's still so much shit to do.* It had started with a pain in the back that wouldn't go away. The doctors had so many questions. Are you a smoker? *Course I am, why do you think I'm coughing?* Do you have chest pains? Have you been losing weight? *Why do ya think I'm here? Asshole.*

And then they'd told him. And McVittie felt like he'd just got kicked in the nuts. *I never thought I'd go this way. Stop feeling sorry for yourself, you old bastard. Look on the bright side, there's still time to clean up a few loose ends.* He wanted to know that Davis was dead, and he wanted to take a few pigs with him. *What a sad old bugger you are*, he thought.

Chapter 28

On Monday morning, Lossan entered the boardroom at Heather Street, feeling surprisingly good, given they were about to embark on another day of interviews. McDonald was already there, sitting with a Styrofoam coffee cup at the end of the table, his white hair sticking up a bit, as though he'd forgotten to comb it in his hurry to get here. Lossan nodded to him and sat on the other side of the table.

A moment later, Kovacs entered, looking grim. "I just got a report from the Vancouver PD—Karl Koehle's body was found in a ditch just outside of New Westminster. Looks like he'd been beaten pretty bad."

"Oh God," said Lossan. "This is going to be the end of George and Thelma Koehle." He rubbed a hand over his face. "I guess I better tell them. One of them is going to have to identify the body. Do you need me here?"

"Go ahead. We'll catch you up when you get back."

"Thanks, Pat. I appreciate this," Kovacs said. And he meant it. The last thing he wanted to deal with was a grieving family. "Before you go. I'm not buying Davis's story that he never profited from the gang's business activities. And I'm still troubled by Davis's photographic memory. I just don't buy it. Too convenient. It's as if he's covering something up. And I want Bolton in the interviews, once we get the records from Davis's cabin."

The other men agreed, and Lossan headed out to meet with the Koehles.

McDonald pressed some of his white fluff against his head and cleared his throat. "All right. Once we go through the records, we should be able to tell how good his memory really is."

***

Lossan was waiting in one of the meeting rooms and wasn't looking forward to giving George Koehle the news. He'd done it many times before, and it was never easy. When George arrived, it seemed as if he knew there was bad news. He didn't say anything, but Lossan could see it in his eyes. Lossan got right to the point.

"George, there's no easy way to say this, but we think we've found Karl's body."

George stood frozen for a full ten seconds. "Could they be wrong, maybe it was someone else?"

"He had his wallet on him. I'm going to need you to come with me to the hospital to identify the body."

"Does Thelma know?"

"We haven't spoken to your wife yet."

George cradled his head in his hands and started to cry. Lossan patted his back awkwardly. "Do you need a bit of time?"

"No, I need to see my son. Let's do it now."

The drive to the morgue took less than five minutes. George looked out the window, having trouble taking it all in. They parked at the rear entrance to the New Westminster hospital, and, within a few minutes, they were walking through some underground tunnels at the hospital to the morgue. The coroner was expecting them. The body was laid out on a viewing table. The coroner walked into the room with Koehle and Lossan. She looked at George and asked if he was ready.

George started to sway and Lossan grabbed him. George then looked at the coroner and nodded. Slowly, she pulled back the sheet cover to reveal his head. George recoiled at first, but when Lossan reached out to him, George found his footing and moved a little closer to the body. Karl looked so peaceful.

Lossan stood back as George bent down and kissed Karl on the forehead. "My boy, my beautiful boy." He stood up straight and looked at Lossan, tears filling his eyes. "Yes, this is my son. This is Karl." Lossan asked him if he wanted a few minutes on his own. George nodded, and Lossan and the coroner left the room.

After a few minutes, George came out. "What am I going to say to Thelma?"

"I don't know, George, but you'll find a way."

"She'll want to see him."

Lossan arranged for another Mountie to tell Thelma the news and bring her to the morgue. Then he waited with the grieving father until she arrived. When she was led into the room, George and Lossan were sitting at a table. Thelma's face was grey, her eyes dull. She didn't look at George but focused on Lossan. "Are ... are you sure?" Her voice was so soft, and something inside George broke when he heard it. He pushed out his chair and moved toward her, his arms stretched out. "I'm sorry, Thelma, I'm so sorry."

Thelma put her hands up and stepped back, her face suddenly red, her eyes flashing. "Don't touch me!"

George started to weep. And all the life seemed to drain out of Thelma again. She took a deep breath and closed her eyes. After what seemed like several minutes, she opened her eyes and said, "I want to see him. I want to see my boy."

Lossan nodded and put an arm out, and Thelma clung to it as they moved through the doors toward her son's body.

***

By the time Lossan returned to the interview with Davis, the afternoon session was almost over, and they were taking a short break before the end of the day. Kovacs updated him. The records that Davis claimed were up at his cabin had been found and were being driven back that afternoon. He was still unconvinced that Davis hadn't benefitted personally from the gang's crimes, but he was starting to appreciate how well he knew the gang's various business operations.

Lossan told him he was exhausted and hadn't realized how emotionally draining breaking the news to George and Thelma had been. He poured himself a glass of water and slumped at the table, trying not to remember the look on Thelma Koehle's face as she stared down at her dead child.

When Davis and Peek returned to the boardroom, they both stared at Lossan. It was obvious something was going on. "They've found Karl Koehle's body," he told them.

"I'm sorry to hear that," Davis said. "Probably thought they could get at George through him…"

Kovacs noticed the hesitation. "Is there something else you want to tell us?"

Davis was thinking back to his conversation with Karl at the restaurant. "Doesn't matter now. But Karl had this crazy idea to stake out Bolton's apartment. Thought Bolton was responsible for his dad's problems and wanted to scare him."

Lossan weighed in. "He must have been the one making the threatening phone calls. And the incident with the girlfriend."

"I don't know about any of that, but Karl was a bit of a loose cannon, hard to control, didn't always listen. Sometimes he would shoot his mouth off."

And now he's dead, thought Lossan. Kovacs looked at the young officer and sighed. "I think we should call it a day," he said.

They decided to reconvene the following morning, once they'd reviewed the records. And Davis was sent back to Oakalla.

✳✳✳

At five o'clock the following morning, four gang members were arrested at their homes. There was no sign of McVittie. Joe Peirson was arrested. He refused to say anything, but Lossan thought the small farm was probably used by the gang pretty regularly to hide assets and people.

Lossan called Bolton. "We think it'd be helpful if you could look at the records we found at Davis's cabin and sit in on our next interview with him."

"You really need me, mate? I'd rather stay out of things now."

Lossan thought he understood. He told him about Karl Koehle, and that it looked likely the kid was the one responsible for scaring his girlfriend and making the phone calls.

Bolton was sorry to hear about Karl, but his interest was piqued and he told Lossan he'd be there in the morning.

Chapter 29

When Bolton arrived at the Heather Street offices, he was shown to one of the upstairs boardrooms. Kovacs showed him the two-inch thick transcript of the Davis interviews, pointed to the records they'd recovered from Davis's cabin and gave him Karl Koehle's medical report.

"You think the gang was responsible for Koehle's death?" Bolton asked.

"Davis said the kid was sticking his nose in too many places. We may never know. Davis will be here in about two hours. Call me on local 156 if you need anything," Kovacs said.

Bolton read the medical report first. It was gruesome and he wished he hadn't read the details. He set the file aside and picked up Davis's statement next, skimming page after page. There was no index. He was looking for names, numbers and dollars. After about forty pages, he read a section on the business ventures, and then a series of names of individuals and businesses that had dealings with the gang. He was having trouble focusing and was about to stop when he came across his own name. Bolton backtracked a few pages and read each line, how Karl Koehle believed that he was responsible for

George's business problems, his idea to stake out of his apartment and the possibility that he may have seen his girlfriend.

Bolton stood up and looked out the window. He was very pale. The thought that this kid could've killed Terry made him sick. He walked to the end of the large table, poured himself a glass of water and sat down. After a few sips, he refocused and pulled the files they'd seized from Davis's cabin toward him. They included bank statements, bank deposit books, cheque stubs, and cash synoptics, and then he noticed a handwritten summary of the cash generated from each business for the last three years. Davis was well organized. He started going through the numerous cash synoptics and was adding up the receipts from each business when Kovacs walked in and said they were ready for Davis.

"I'm only halfway through the records and—"

"You'll have time to finish that later. Let's go."

Davis looked surprised when Bolton walked in the room.

"I hope you don't mind, we asked Paul Bolton to join us," Kovacs said, sitting down across from Davis.

Peek looked at Kovacs and then Bolton. "It's unusual. If he's just an observer, then the questions have to be asked by either you or Corporal Lossan."

"That's fine," Kovacs said.

Bolton looked at Davis and wondered what he knew about Terry.

Kovacs said, "We'd like to talk about the money. Where did it all go, eh?"

Davis replied, "Most of it's still there, in bank accounts or real estate. McVittie took almost nothing out of any of the businesses, and for someone scared of banks, he had a lot of trust in them. I told him to look at offshore banks, set up a trust, invest in real estate. He said he wanted to keep it simple."

Davis went on to describe each business, but it was clear the drug business was the biggest and the others were simply used to recycle the drug money. Davis didn't come across as conceited or arrogant. It all sounded so simple; he knew each of the businesses intimately and spoke for almost an hour without interruption.

Kovacs looked over at Bolton from time to time and noticed he was taking notes. Every now and again, someone would ask a question. Davis would listen quietly and respond calmly. After about three hours, Peek and Davis moved to another room for lunch while the rest of them stayed in the boardroom. They all grabbed sandwiches and coffee. Kovacs looked at Bolton. "What do you think? You believe him?"

Bolton looked down at his notes and thought for a few moments before answering. "He's very organized, has an excellent memory." He looked up at Kovacs. "He'll make a great witness. But I have to say, I'm surprised the money is still all there." He shifted one of the files toward Kovacs and ran his pen down a page. "Look at all this. Roughly ninety million in cash at sixteen different banks and credit unions, along with residential properties. And what I really don't understand is how Davis could have worked for a tosser like McVittie for so long."

Kovacs shook his head, "What are you getting at?"

"It's not just the money," Bolton said. "They're really nothing alike. Davis had a chance to get rid of George Koehle, but he didn't. Now he's risking his own life to testify against the gang."

Kovacs just stared at him for moment, his ham sandwich forgotten in his hand. "Who cares? They're all criminals."

Bolton thought back to the first time he met Davis at George's office. Sometimes people didn't have a choice, sometimes you only saw their real character in times of adversity. Maybe Davis was someone who could change, and maybe, when confronted with tough decisions, he could make the right choice after all. "I'd like to finish reading Davis's earlier statements and complete my review of the records. I want to understand how he ended up in the gang and why he didn't kill George."

"Suit yourself," Kovacs said.

When the interview wrapped up for the day, Bolton asked if he could use the room and continue his review of the records and Davis's statements. It was close to 9:00 p.m. before he finished. He would review his extensive notes that evening and bring them back with him for the morning session that was scheduled for 9:30 a.m.

***

Davis had just finished his evening meal when there was a knock on his cell door. The guard announced it was time for his evening stroll. As his cell door opened, he looked up at an unfamiliar face. "Where's the other guy?" Davis asked.

"Sick. Let's go."

Davis got up from his chair and followed the guard out. He went to the courtyard the same way every evening. Once there, he was free to walk around the yard, which was shaped like a baseball diamond and lit up by large floodlights. The guard sat on a bench in the shadows, about thirty feet to the left of the entrance. Davis couldn't see him, but he knew the guy was watching.

The perimeter was about three hundred steps, and Davis usually did fifteen laps, which took about thirty minutes. He was about thirty steps past the bench on his third lap when he heard a sigh. He looked back at the bench but couldn't see anything.

Slowly, Davis retraced his steps. As he got closer, he noticed the guard slumped down to one side. The hairs on the back of Davis's neck stood up. He looked around. No one in sight. He slowly walked up to the guard, kicked his feet. No reaction. He kicked him harder. Still nothing, but Davis was close enough to see his eyes were closed. He glanced around again, then bent down and shook the guard, but the man only slumped down even further. Davis was still leaning over when he heard a movement behind him. He turned just as an arm swung at him and something sharp pierced his abdomen just below the rib cage.

He'd been in enough bar fights to know it was a stiletto. He fell backwards and tried to roll out of the way. As he stood up, he felt a sharp pain. He brought his hand to his stomach and felt a dampness. With the light behind him, Davis could see his attacker: over six feet tall and well-built, holding the stiletto in the palm of his outstretched hand. Davis held his damaged stomach with his left hand and used the other for balance as he took small steps backwards. The attacker circled, forcing Davis back toward the wall.

The attacker lunged again, missing him by inches. Davis swung his right fist hard into the side of the other man's temple. His attacker was stunned but didn't fall. He turned the stiletto in his hand and aimed it at Davis's chest. Davis knew how to fight dirty—he rushed forward and, just as the other man raised his right hand, Davis kicked him hard in the groin. As his assailant keeled over, Davis jumped on top of him, grabbing his right wrist with both hands. The guy was strong and grabbed Davis's throat with his massive left hand, squeezing his windpipe. Davis sank his teeth into his attacker's right hand and heard a scream as the stiletto fell to the ground. Davis grabbed the weapon and plunged it into the side of the other man's throat. Blood spurted everywhere. He rolled off his attacker, gasping for air and, within a few seconds, passed out.

***

It was after 11:00 p.m. before anyone noticed the guard missing.

By 11:30, they found him slumped on the bench, no pulse. A prisoner lay on the ground nearby with a stiletto sticking out of the side of his neck; he'd been dead for a while. Another prisoner lay on his back, eyes closed and a large circle of blood just below his rib cage.

At midnight, Kovacs got the call. He was up and out of his house before 12:15 a.m.

***

Kovacs and Lossan met at Vancouver General Hospital. Davis was still in surgery when they arrived. The news wasn't good: Davis had lost a lot of blood, his vital signs were poor, and they were worried about damage to internal organs or possible severing of an artery. He was expected to be in surgery for at least two hours and there wouldn't be any news for a while. They were told to come back in the morning.

They drove together to Oakalla, where the warden met them at the entrance, holding a cup of coffee and looking like he was not impressed he'd been dragged out of bed in the middle of the night. What little hair he had left was fluffed up around his ears and he hadn't bothered to brush his teeth. He slugged back his coffee and motioned to an adjacent room where the prison doctor and the guards that found Davis were already seated at a small table.

Warden Smith introduced the doctor and the guards who stood up. He yawned and set his mug down before finally looking at them both. "Well, as far as we know, Davis was exercising in the courtyard around 8:40 p.m. The guard on duty was new; poor bastard just started a week ago."

"What happened to the regular guard?" asked Lossan.

"Called in sick," Smith said.

Kovacs stared at the man. "Was this Davis's regular exercise time?"

Smith scratched his nose. "Yup. Every night. The yard was empty. All prisoners have to be inside by 8:00 p.m. Davis walks alone after that. I can't figure how another prisoner got into the courtyard."

"Perhaps he had help," Kovacs said.

Smith glared at him. But both Lossan and Kovacs knew there wasn't much he could say. All indications pointed to someone on the inside assisting the prisoner.

"Doctor," Lossan said, turning toward a tall man with glasses. "Can you tell us what you found?"

The doctor explained that the guard had been stabbed close to the carotid artery. "Probably dead in a matter of seconds." He went on to say that Davis's wound was quite deep. His assailant meant to kill him.

"What are Davis's chances?" Kovacs asked.

"I've no idea how much blood he lost or whether there was damage to his internal organs. But I'd say it's lucky he was still alive when we found him. Someone was watching over him last night."

Lossan looked at the two guards. "We got a murder weapon?"

"We found a six-inch stiletto still in the dead prisoner's neck. It mighta been used to kill our guy too," said the taller guard.

Kovacs had a lot on his mind. He turned and walked out, leaving Lossan to thank the men. As he caught up with him at the entrance to the prison, Lossan said, "So, McVittie's got someone in here."

"No doubt about it. The prisoner killing that young guard, though…"

Lossan glanced at the older cop. "Sounds like he wasn't the one in on it."

Kovacs stayed silent. But he was thinking the same thing. Someone else set this up.

Chapter 30

The van had been parked across the street from the house for three days. The officer inside was restless. He kicked a scrunched-up fast-food wrapper out of his way as he stretched his long legs in front of him. It had been another long night. He yawned and was about to pour his third coffee when someone walked onto the driveway, looked around, then put a key in the door, opened it and entered the house. The officer set his cup down, pushed a few more wrappers out of his way and found the phone number for Corporal Lossan's home.

"Pat, it's Wally. I'm outside McVittie's house now. Looks like he's home."

It had been two days since the attack on Davis, and Lossan was still catching up on his sleep. He'd wondered if McVittie would show up, assuming it was him and not one of his lackeys. He doubted they'd try and go after Davis in the hospital, but like Kovacs, he wouldn't put anything past him.

Lossan looked at his watch. It was 5:00 a.m. "You sure, Wally?"

"The picture's pretty grainy and it's still dark, but someone just used a key to go inside."

"Okay. Stay put, I'll be there in twenty minutes. Oh, and call dispatch. Have someone coordinate support in case he leaves the house."

Lossan called the RCMP Emergency Response Team and then Kovacs before grabbing his coat and running out the door. He arrived within fifteen minutes, parked a ways down the street, and sidled quickly to the far side of the van. He knocked on the back door and climbed in as soon as it was opened. "Jesus, Wally. It's a mess in here."

"I was hungry. I've been here three days, you know." Wally brushed a few wrappers off the steel table supporting the computer monitors. "Here, take a look at this." Wally had three pictures up on his screen: one covering the front door, one covering the street and one covering the backyard. "He's still in there."

A few minutes later, there was a tap on the van door and the ERT leader climbed in. Larry Jackson was a huge man with a deep voice that usually made everyone look up when he started speaking. This moment was no different. "My team will sweep the front and back of the house and close off the street. He alone?"

"No one's been in or out since I've been here and that's three days now," Wally said.

There was another tap on the door and Kovacs joined them in the van, which was getting very crowded.

"All right," Jackson said. "We'll make contact and ask him to surrender peacefully." Kovacs couldn't help snorting. Jackson ignored this and continued his speech. "Failing that, we'll try and contain him. Is he armed? Could he have explosives in the house?"

"Definitely armed," Kovacs said. "And I wouldn't rule out explosives."

***

McVittie couldn't remember ever being so angry. He'd cursed George Koehle's name all the way home from the cabin. And then he cursed Davis. The traitor. The attempt on his life had failed. Could nothing go right? And he hadn't been able to get hold of Charlie Coulson, which meant he had to come all the way back to the city to take care of Davis. He knew with his shitty leg he'd not be much good at slipping in and out of hospital without being noticed. He'd arranged to meet up with a few of the boys. They could deal with Davis.

There wasn't much time. Davis would be heavily guarded. He needed his guns, his passport and some cash. McVittie pulled his sore leg along with him to the kitchen counter and picked up the phone. Five minutes later, he slammed it down for the third time. The few contacts still answering their phones told him police were everywhere, watching everyone, and some of the gang had already been picked up by the police. But at this point, McVittie had nothing to lose. In some ways, he hoped they'd be watching the place.

With a groan, he headed to the basement and grabbed what he needed. His breathing was heavy as he made his way back up the steps, half pulling himself on the railing. He'd go out the back door and take the long way to his car. As he opened the curtain to look out, he caught some movement at the edge of the garden. He stood there for a full minute just watching. Then he saw it. A shadow. Police were already there. He went to the front of the house and pulled the curtain back a few inches. He could barely make out three men dressed head to toe in black uniforms and armed with semi-automatic weapons across the street, next to a black van.

McVittie wasn't about to spend his last month in prison. He pulled out a flashlight and opened his bag. He took out the two Glocks and put one in each pocket. He took out the AK-47. He'd go out the front door, the police wouldn't expect that. He'd take out as many of them as he could before he went down.

McVittie slowly opened the door, took a few seconds to focus, and lifted the AK-47 as he stepped outside. He got off ten shots before he was hit twice in the upper chest. He was still falling to the ground when a further hail of bullets sliced into him.

Chapter 31

When Kovacs and Lossan visited Davis, he was still a little drowsy from the medication. Lossan smiled at him. "You had us worried there for a while."

Davis tried to raise himself and winced in pain. He looked up and tried to focus. "Any sign of McVittie?"

Kovacs smirked. "We met up with him early this morning back at his house."

"I imagine he didn't go quietly."

"You could say that. He came out his front door firing an AK-47. Hit three policemen before he was shot dead." Kovacs crushed his Styrofoam coffee cup and tossed it into the trash can.

"Good to see you're taking care of your assets." Davis lay back in his bed and wondered why McVittie did that. He probably didn't want to go to prison again.

***

It was almost two weeks before Davis was able to attend more police interviews. Crown counsel prepared charges against the five gang members. Coulson was captured and charged with conspiracy to commit murder, false imprisonment and threatening a witness. He and four other gang members were charged with importation and trafficking of illegal drugs, failure to remit duties and taxes on imports, money laundering and failure to pay income taxes.

Kovacs hoped to secure convictions against senior officials at the Port of Vancouver, as well as Vancouver residents with ties to Mexican and Colombian drug cartels. The conspiracy to commit murder charge depended on Joe Peirson's evidence. Given that the gang members were his so-called friends, and he had a mental capacity of a ten year old, everyone knew that the murder charge was dead in the water. Peirson claimed he was taking care of Karl Koehle while he was at the farm. He admitted to knowing several gang members and allowing them to use his farm to store goods and have the occasional party. He denied chaining Koehle to a wall in one of his piggeries or harming him in any way. He claimed he'd helped Charlie Coulson load Karl into the back of Coulson's truck, so he could be taken to a hospital, and that Koehle was still alive when he left the farm, because he heard him groaning.

The initial search of the farm revealed a pigsty where there was a series of chains attached to a wall. Inside the farmhouse, the police found a pair of metal ankle and hand restraints. The officers that interviewed Peirson questioned his mental capacity. As their only witness, the conspiracy to commit murder charge looked weak.

The RCMP Security Service obtained an order freezing all the gang's bank accounts and other assets, including seven lower mainland residences. The assets had an approximate value of ninety million dollars. All the residences were rented out to offshore tenants whose children were attending school or college in Vancouver.

***

A few days later, Lossan phoned Kovacs and suggested they get together for a drink. They met in a bar in Gastown not far from

Carrall Street, where they'd first met. Lossan was already seated at a table when Kovacs walked in. He'd even ordered a whisky for Kovacs. The two cops sat amiably at the table and sipped their drinks.

"So, what's next for you?" Lossan asked.

Kovacs took a sip and set his glass down. "Just handed in my papers. This time next month, I'll be on a beach in Los Cabos. Then retirement, maybe somewhere on the island."

Lossan was happy for the old guy. "You'll miss it."

No, Kovacs thought, *I've been doing this for too long.* Today there was more red tape, more rules, more gangs and less political will to tackle the problem. Crime had become global and complex. They needed dedicated resources, specialized task forces. They needed to change the way they prosecuted. Most of all, they needed to start infiltrating gangs. Kovacs sighed. "Today's criminals are smarter, more sophisticated. They get other criminals to help them, and it's tougher to find the assets."

"Isn't that what Davis was telling us?" Lossan asked.

Kovacs grimaced. "Yeah, he was wasting his time with those guys. It's time for a new breed, you hear it everywhere. The guy gets off because he has a good lawyer, the evidence is inadmissible, the wiretap illegal. We're more concerned about protecting a criminal's rights than putting him away."

***

A few months later, McDonald, the gang prosecutor, called to congratulate Lossan on his role in the joint investigation with the RCMP Security Service.

Lossan smiled into the phone. "Have you made any progress against the longshoremen and those connected to the Port of Vancouver?"

McDonald sighed on the other end of the phone. "We're running into political pressure from the feds. I can only assume that means the case has been dropped. Someone back east is … shall we say, covering their backside and trying to slow down or maybe even prevent an inquiry into the management of the Port authority." Lossan could picture him scratching his white beard. "Oh, and Lossan, I sent you a copy of the press release being issued tomorrow."

Lossan thanked him and hung up. He glanced down at the release he'd received that morning:

Inspector Hatley, BC head of the RCMP's Commercial Crime Division, is pleased to announce that after months of a joint criminal investigation with the RCMP Security Service, the provincial Crown has secured convictions against several members of a Vancouver gang. The sentences range from eight to fifteen years and will be served in maximum security prisons in Eastern Canada. The charges relate to conspiracy to commit murder, drug trafficking, illegal importation of banned substances and failure to pay taxes. The Crown seized bank accounts and other assets that in value represent the second largest recovery of crime proceeds in the country in the last ten years. The successful prosecution of these crimes is the result of many months of hard work by several members of the RCMP Security Service and the Commercial Crime Division of the RCMP.

Chapter 32

Two years later

Thelma Koehle supported her husband when they buried their son, Karl. She supported him through the trial. Even when they lost their house, she supported him. Even when the church elders shunned her and told her she wasn't welcome, she stayed with him.

She and George were relocated to a small town in rural southern Saskatchewan under the federal witness protection program. She spent her days reading the Bible and looking for meaning in all that had happened. She read articles in the church's magazine, *Awake*, about forgiveness, anxiety, depression and how to cope with major life crises. Forgiveness is a personal choice, the article told her. Anger and bitterness sour relationships, leading to isolation and loneliness. Forgiveness leads to healthier relationships, empathy, understanding and compassion. Thelma did not feel understanding or compassion. But she tried.

She found some comfort in the Bible. One passage from Colossians reminded her to forgive, as the Lord forgave you. Again, she struggled with this, especially given her church's decision to shun her and George. And then, her way became suddenly clear. It was as if she'd woken from a dream.

A month after being relocated, she left her husband and went to live with her sister in northern Alberta. Her sister was also a member of the church and encouraged her to apply for reinstatement. The church elders contacted Thelma's old church in Vancouver. Thelma was told that disfellowshipped individuals may be reinstated into the congregation if they were considered repentant. Thelma applied and waited. The Vancouver elders were still determining whether she had repented.

Finally, they sent out their report. It stated that while she wasn't responsible for the conduct of her husband, separation from her husband was in contravention of their beliefs. However, there were mitigating circumstances. She was required to attend meetings while still being shunned as a condition of her eventual reinstatement. In addition, she was required to volunteer and promote the Watch Tower Bible and Tract Society and attend bible classes.

While no specific period of time was prescribed for her reinstatement, she was told it would be reviewed in a year.

***

George was in counselling at Saskatoon City Hospital. For the last year he'd been working as a part-time hospital porter. Slowly, he was adjusting to life alone. Encouraged by his counsellor, he developed an interest in wildlife. One of his co-workers was a keen ornithologist and suggested he come along to Last Mountain Lake. It was the oldest bird sanctuary in North America and an important migratory stopover for hundreds of thousands of birds travelling between their northern breeding grounds and their southern wintering grounds.

George and his friend drove two hours southwest of Saskatoon in the hopes of seeing some of the almost three hundred species of birds, including endangered birds like the peregrine falcon, the piping plover, the burrowing owl and, the tallest, the whooping crane—one of the rarest birds in the world. His friend told him that a common tern that had been banded there in 1956 was recovered 12,000 kilometres away, in the Cook Islands, in 1960. It was a long trip. But once they got to the lake, George was glad he'd come. He got out of the car and stretched, staring out at the sandy shoreline. They hiked for three hours, watching birds and visitors and boats.

He wondered if his interest in wildlife started when he'd spent time up in northern BC with Alan Davis. The only drawback to his new pastime was that it was somewhat lonely. Trips like this, with a friend, were rare. And he hadn't enjoyed the long, cold winter last year. He knew he'd hate it again this year. Unlike Vancouver, where you'd have rain for six months, in the prairies, it was snow. The winter nights were long and lonely. He needed to get out more and he needed some sunshine. George thought back to his trips to Hawaii.

And he thought a lot about Thelma and Karl. He knew he wasn't a good role model and regretted not doing a better job as a father and a husband. He looked back on his own childhood and realized it wasn't much different. His counsellor told him that he'd been though some very traumatic events, not only loss of his son and his wife, but also his business, which had become a big part of his life. He needed to think about what he enjoyed in life. George decided he would do just that.

***

Paul Bolton's life had calmed down a lot since the days of working with Lossan and Kovacs, and he wasn't sorry. He looked across the room at Terry, who was on the phone with a friend, laughing, and he smiled. He'd asked her to move in right after the whole Koehle thing was finished, and he'd never been happier. He did miss the excitement a bit, though.

The federal government was talking about tackling corruption at the country's major ports. Bolton's ears had pricked up when Lossan had called earlier that week and told him about it. Maybe they'd work together again after all.

***

Ryan Kelly was finally enjoying the quiet life, the life he'd longed for, a life in the wilderness. He kept mostly to himself, and he'd grown a beard, but it had taken a long time before he stopped looking over his shoulder.

This was his second full season as a fishing guide on the Miramichi River, which ran into the Atlantic and was world famous for its fly fishing. The groups were never more than two at a time, but he never made small talk. He knew he'd make more money in tips if he did. But that was part of his new life.

Kelly lived in a cabin eight kilometres away, on a small, isolated lake—one road in and one road out. He knew he'd have to move at some point, one day it would happen, but he didn't think it would be this quickly. The message had been pinned to the board. He asked the manager who'd called.

"No idea. Just wanted to know if you still worked here. Didn't leave a name or number."

Kelly stared at the message. They knew where he was. He had a number he could call if something like this happened. There was still a week left in the season. He thought about packing up and heading out that day. He'd always known, sooner or later they'd find him.

***

A tall man walked into the arrivals lounge at Moncton airport, waved at his contact and crossed the room toward him. "You missed the connection, it's iffy at the best of times," the contact told him.

The tall man checked into a motel about twenty minutes from the airport and changed his clothes. He planned to be at the lodge around 2:30 p.m. The directions were pretty simple. Turn off at Shediac and head north on Highway 11 along the Acadian Coast.

Once he left Moncton, all he could see on the side of the highway were trees. Not the size of the trees on the West Coast, these were like matchsticks. The towns en route were all in French or Mi'kmaq: le Pays de la Sagouine, Kouchibouguac National Park. He saw a lot of large trucks on the highway and knew if he kept on it, he'd hit the Quebec border. The trucks kept thundering down the hills but laboured on the long, slow, gradual uphill sections.

When he pulled into the lodge, there was no one around. He walked down to the small dock. The cabins were old and looked pretty basic. He was about to head back to the car, thinking he'd have to come back early the following morning, when an old man walked toward him. The tall man asked if he knew where he could find Ryan Kelly.

"Who wants to know?"

"A buddy of mine fished here a year ago and recommended him. I'm just travelling through and thought I might see if he had some time to take me out."

"He's done for the day. Try the morning. Early, mind you. He's usually out by seven."

"Where would I find him right now?"

"Probably gone home. Lives up the road a ways. Place called Blackville—hang on…" The old man squinted a bit and pointed. "That looks like him now, in the red truck."

Kelly felt bad about leaving with a week still to go and wanted to say goodbye to the few friends he'd made at the lodge. He saw the manager talking to a stranger down by the dock. The stranger turned around and started to walk toward him. Kelly reached into the glove compartment and pulled out his gun. The stranger was about thirty feet away when Kelly opened his door. Still holding his gun by his side, he got out and stood behind the door. The stranger looked familiar, but he couldn't place him.

"Mr. Kelly, I've been looking for you."

Kelly moved from behind the door, raised his gun and pointed it at the stranger. "Don't come any closer."

The tall man put his hands up. "Whoa … I just want to talk to you. Don't you recognize me?"

Kelly shook his head.

"It's Lossan, Pat Lossan. Don't you remember?"

So that's who called the other day. "What do you want?"

Lossan smiled. "Do you mind lowering the gun?" Lossan waited for Kelly to comply. Then he smiled as he walked up to Alan Davis. "We have a proposition for you. Is there somewhere private we can talk?"

Davis led Lossan into the lodge and headed to the back office. He opened a cabinet and pulled out a bottle of whisky and two tumblers, then sat down and took a long swig. "Sit down. Drink?"

"Looks like you're the one that needs the drink. What's with the gun?"

"Let's just say you weren't who I was expecting."

Lossan proceeded to explain the reason for his visit. He told him that the RCMP Security Service had been working on a plan to tackle the drug problem at the Montreal port and Davis's name came up. With the change of government, there was a renewed desire and will to tackle the stranglehold that organized crime had on the ports and to break the unions handling cargo. They wanted someone with first-hand knowledge, someone that thought like a criminal. An insider, if you will. They knew it was a long shot, but they thought they'd try.

Davis poured himself another drink. He was sure his past had caught up with him, and in a way, it had. He felt relieved, he felt wanted. He took a slow drink of whisky and started to think about what he wanted to do with the rest of his life. He wanted to be someone his daughter would be proud of. An hour ago, he was running away. Is that what he wanted to do for the rest of his life?

Lossan carried on talking while Davis thought about what he really wanted to do. Some of the RCMP Security Service's ideas didn't make sense, but he liked the thought of becoming some sort of adviser. He knew they had to infiltrate the gangs, penetrate the unions, even management. Davis didn't want to just survive; he wanted to live, to become someone. He needed to use his brains and his skills. And he wanted a chance at redemption. He set his glass down. He wanted to see his daughter. He wondered what she was doing and what she looked like. She'd be fifteen now.

Maybe it was time to take some risks again. Maybe, this time, he'd get it right and be able to help people and make his daughter proud. But most of all he wanted to do it for himself.

He looked up into Lossan's smiling face and told him he'd think about it. But one thing he knew for sure, he wouldn't be back at Miramichi next year.

Acknowledgements

My appreciation to Janet Williamson and David McNeil for their help and encouragement in the early stages. My thanks to all the people at Iguana Books who made this happen, especially Paula Chiarcos, Amanda Feeney and Heather Bury for their hard work, and Greg Ioannou for his vision.

CPSIA information can be obtained
at www.ICGtesting.com
Printed in the USA
BVHW031407210821
614242BV00003B/8